Children
of
Pithiviers

Children
of
Pithiviers

→>-<←

Sheila Kohler

Z
ZOLAND BOOKS
Cambridge, Massachusetts

First edition published in 2001 by
Zoland Books, Inc.
384 Huron Avenue
Cambridge, Massachusetts 02138

Portions of this novel appeared,
in somewhat different form, in
Fiction (Chapter 5) and *Conjunctions* (Chapter 4).

FIRST EDITION

Book design by Boskydell Studio
Printed in the United States of America

05 04 03 02 01   8 7 6 5 4 3 2 1

This book is printed on acid-free paper, and its binding
materials have been chosen for strength and durability.

Library of Congress Cataloging-in-Publication Data
Kohler, Sheila.
The children of pithiviers : a novel / Sheila Kohler.
p. cm.
ISBN 1-58195-032-2
1. Aristocracy (Social class) — Fiction. 2. Pithiviers (France) — Fiction.
3. Jewish children — Fiction. 4. Teenage girls — Fiction. I. Title.
PR9369.3.K64 C47 2001
823'.914 — dc21
00-068549

*This book is for the children who passed
through the camps of Pithiviers
and Beaune-la-Rolande and were
sent on to the gas chambers.*

We estimate that there are about four thousand Jewish children from the ages of two to fourteen in the camps at Pithiviers and Beaune-la-Rolande in the occupied zone. The care given them is altogether insufficient and the conditions of hygiene deplorable. There is only one supervisor for fifty children. According to the information we have received these children will be deported, and we believe their identity cards will be removed before their deportation. As far as we know the fate of these children depends entirely upon the French government. Several Jewish associations have offered to assume the costs of caring for these children if they are put into their hands.

Mr. Tuck, American Chargé d'Affaires
August 1942

Part One

1

IT WAS ONE SENTENCE that struck me. It was not the sort of sentence one would forget entirely, left in the margin of someone else's book. Not that I knew what the sentence was referring to at the time. And even when I did know, I did not fully comprehend; it took years to do that.

Mother said everything would be all right; nothing seriously wrong can happen in France: is it not the country of the Rights of Man?

The place, Pithiviers, lies in what is known as the breadbasket of France. I first saw it in the late fifties, as you can see it today, as the children must have seen it when they came there from Paris in the summer of '42.

It is the country! the country! The sun shines down on wide wheat fields. A sweet breeze blows as if from the sea. Sunflowers lift up their big heads on dry stalks. Glossy crows gorge themselves on green wheat. In the distance, a church spire pierces the pale blue sky.

The big sky, the vast, flat places, the freedom of it all,

brought my home to mind. I noted the names of the small towns on the signs or the well-marked roads. I smiled at names like Thignonville and Lolainville.

The driver indicated the place where I was to descend, and I made my way forward from the back of the bus, skating my hand over the plush seats with their white antimacassars, going past a laughing couple. A young girl — she must have been hardly older than I was — sat entwined with an older man: her arm slung around his shoulders, her leg over his leg. The girl was gazing up at him with dewy eyes, and she was giggling and squirming in her seat. Her plump, glistening lips begged for a kiss. He bent down to her, and I could not stop myself from watching as she opened her mouth to his tongue with the greediness of a famished child.

I was thinking of the young man I had left in Paris.

What could a girl of her age see in a man of his? Did she find him attractive? Yes she did. Yes she did.

I glanced at the man with something akin to dislike. Not only was he old in my eyes but he was dressed like a young man, and smiled down at the girl with a disdainful half smile. He wore dark glasses, the kind that curve to cover the sides of one's face, almost like a mask. His skin was smooth and slightly pink, but it was clearly the skin of an old man. His tight trousers might have looked elegant on someone younger. Reddish hair fell onto his forehead in two greasy curls. I turned away.

Years later, traveling on another bus through Long Island, I saw a very similar old man, pretending to be young, wearing identical glasses. He was probably going to his house in the Hamptons. He pushed his glasses up onto his head as though he wished to see me better, or so that I could see his red-rimmed eyes. He gave me a stare, and I half-expected him to say, "Have fun, sweetheart," as the Frenchman had done, his words causing me a disturbance, an inner throb, like the tightening of some long-unused muscle.

Then I was in the light, trudging painfully in tight, high-heeled shoes, going through wheat fields to the top of a hill, with my heavy backpack, my head lowered, gaze down, toiling along the hard, dry path the bus driver had indicated.

I felt a weight on my heart. I was wide open to the rooks' caw-cawing, to the brightness in the air. There was the solemn hush, the strange dreamlike clarity of the out-lines of things. I wanted nothing so much as to kick off my shoes, hitch up my tight skirt, remove my stockings, and return along the pathway to wait for the next bus back to Paris; but, as in a dream, I was dragged onward by some-thing, curiosity, the need to know what would happen next.

Besides, I knew I would not be welcome back in Paris. I had been packed off in disgrace. "How could you shame us so?" they had said, though at the time I did it, I had not thought it shameful at all.

I had had little choice but to follow my sister's sugges-tion that I leave for the country immediately, though I did not see why, at seventeen, I had to wear her high heels and a black dress. "I'll look as if I'm going to a funeral, Cecile.

And anyway, we've paid in advance, haven't we?" I had said.

"First impressions," my sister had insisted. "You want to have a good time, don't you, darling?" she said. She had put her arms around me and held me close, and I had boarded the bus. By the end of the '50s you could get to that place only by car or bus, though there must once have been a train; I later came across train tracks in the long grass that led nowhere.

There was the dull sound of my shoes in the sand, the keening of the wind that blows constantly across those fields, and the faint murmur of the river that would become part of all my troubled dreams. I stood at the top of the hill and surveyed the scene: the trembling leaves, the clear water gliding under the mill, the white roses growing wild along the fence. I breathed in the smell of the sun on the slow-moving water, of the roses, of the June afternoon, of the beginning of things.

The dust path descended steeply between tall poplars into the green valley. A low stone wall protected the evenly graveled forecourt, with its beds of moon roses on either side, from the road. Behind the courtyard the old stone, creeper-covered mill straddled the river, though there was no longer any wheel. The mill lay surrounded by a large garden, through which the river meandered idly. Silver willows, not the weeping kind, lined its banks and seemed to stir up the pale sky. The river was a small tributary of the Loire, called l'Oeuf.

The first person I saw on entering the courtyard was a slim, dark-haired man with a mustache, wearing tight, dark clothes. He slunk, catlike, but limping slightly, along the wall. He turned his head, stared at me solemnly, unblinking, and disappeared into the darkness of the garage.

When I lifted the knocker and let it fall against the green door, the only reply was the sound of furious barking. A big dog, I could see through the square panes of the door, leaped up and hurled himself against the door, scraping his paws against the glass, and then ran back and forth in the hall. I stood back and looked up at the house. Was this the right place? Was I not expected? The small panes of the windows glinted blindly in the early afternoon light.

Could there be other mills nearby? Yes, it was an area of mills, of granges, and of inland waterways to carry the wheat away. But yes, yes, someone was coming.

A stout, sallow woman with a squint opened the door, holding on to the dog, which I was afraid would otherwise have devoured me alive. She shouted at him in accented French and asked me in a similar tone what I wanted.

I inquired in my best French if this was the Moulin du Roi, where I was to be a paying guest, waving the advertisement from *Le Figaro* in her face and pronouncing my name. She squinted darkly at the piece of paper and then to one side of me. Because of the squint she never seemed to be looking directly at me but at some invisible double at my side.

She said sourly that this place was named Duruy, and that there was no king around here, never had been, as far as she knew, and she should know, after all, as she had been living here for some twenty years. I suggested the paper had misprinted the advertisement.

After that she left me standing uneasily in the sun. I listened to the cry of the crows and the whisper of the slow-flowing water.

The hall was cool, with its black-and-white flagstones, whitewashed walls, and low-beamed ceiling. The door to the cloakroom stood ajar, and I could see tall daisies through the window.

The woman, whom I learned later was the cook, Dolores, released the dog and retreated down a long corridor, disappearing into a dimly lit kitchen. Now that we were acquainted, the dog ignored me and trotted through the open glass doors into the salon, where he jumped onto the Louis Quinze sofa and looked up, watching the staircase with his ears pricked and the dark, sorrowful gaze of a doomed soul. I followed him into the vast room.

In contrast to the hall's low ceiling, the ceiling of the salon soared, and reaching up to it, long windows opened on the garden and the warm air. A round window, high up a wall, stared down like the unblinking eye of some huge beast. A series of etchings of famous pugilists in bellicose poses, fists lifted, feet apart, knees bent, lined the staircase, and an inlaid cupboard in the corner of the room displayed pieces of fine but chipped porcelain; three delicate armchairs faced the sofa before a large, empty fireplace, where the ashes from some long-cold fire were still piled in the grate. Oilcloth covered the faded fleur-de-lis-patterned upholstery like shrouds.

The elegance of that room always made me uneasy. Did I notice it at first? Or was it only later that I became aware of the dark marks of paintings no longer hanging on the walls, of the faint stains around the edges of the silk curtains, a dimness that suggested something slightly soiled?

I drew cautiously nearer to the dog and gingerly stroked his head, muttering *"Joli chien,"* or something of that sort, all the French flattery I could muster. I had learned French from a Belgian woman at boarding school, then polished it at the Sorbonne for three months, but it was still at the rudimentary stage.

The dog lifted his head and pricked up his ears as together we watched Madame, as I came to call my hostess, descend the main staircase, looking down at me. A small, slender woman, her glasses in one hand, she nevertheless conveyed an idea of height, by holding her head high, her back straight. Though no longer young — at first I thought she must have been in her early 40s — she was handsome, with features that seemed from another age: the high forehead, the pale coloring, the fine bones. But it was her eyes that struck me particularly. They were blue, wide-spaced, very large and melancholy. The upper lids were heavy, as if weighted.

I presumed I had woken her from a nap, for she was wearing a long, flowing negligee, with ruffles and a bow around the neck. Or did she plan to greet me in that way? Her hair was tied so neatly back from her pointed face that when she flicked an imaginary curl behind her ears with her almond-shaped nails, it seemed unnecessary. She wore beige leather slippers with porcelain heels, which clicked and sucked as she descended the stairs. She floated toward me, her walk extraordinarily graceful, light and proud and delicate, though she eyed me with a rather remote expression that I thought might make people hesitate to approach her in the street.

She gestured toward the sofa and sat down next to me. From time to time she casually stroked her brown dog — a *braque allemand*, she called him, who lay alertly at her feet as we spoke. Her voice had interesting pitches, little dips and rises, high notes and husky undertones that sounded almost like the water murmuring beneath her mill. Her French, though fast, was easy to understand, because she spoke with the hint of an English accent and even used certain English words, which I thought at first were for my benefit but afterward discovered were considered elegant among people of her class.

Taken aback by her proximity on the small sofa, by her smooth flow of French words, I found it difficult to focus on what she was saying. The effort made me feel very tired, and made my head throb. I sat up very straight, balanced precariously on a corner of the sofa, my poor, aching feet side by side. She asked me several questions in rapid succession, her head tilted slightly in gracious inquiry, her fine eyebrows arched, her hands clasped, her gaze fixed brightly on my face as on some fascinating spectacle, listening as though rapt, supplying the missing words from time to time in my laborious sentences. Not possessing the precise word, I was obliged to resort to circumlocutions.

I was not used to the art of conversation, and I believed she was concerned for my well-being, absorbed by my halting story. She had the capacity to appear entirely engrossed by my words. I thought she was inordinately glad to have me there, and wondered then, a little, why she was. She leaned so close toward me that I felt she might touch me. I told her I had spent most of my life away from home in boarding school, because my mother had been unwell, a euphemism I half-believed at the time. I confessed that I was afraid of missing my elder sister, but that she was preoccupied with her little boy, her doctor husband, her advanced pregnancy. I said that I was happy to find myself in the countryside after three months in Paris, as I had found the city confusing, the Parisians hard and often rude. Naturally, I did not say anything about Richard, about my disgrace.

As if she had read my mind, she asked me if I had any suitors, and whether any of them might visit me here. I lowered my gaze and felt myself flush and shook my head. "Never mind," she said, putting her hand very gently on my arm, "you are bound to meet more interesting people with us," and a smile flickered across her face so fast I thought I might have imagined it. It reminded me of a day in the Île-de-France, lovely when lit up but, like the sunlight there, ephemeral. I found it impossible not to respond to her smile with a smile.

I listened carefully as she told me flatly, as though it were something she had often recited, that I would be served breakfast in bed, tea in the afternoon on the lawn, weather permitting, and supper with the family, if there were no guests, of course. I would have to manage for myself at lunch. There was always plenty of bread and cheese. Americans — as far as she was concerned all non-Europeans were Americans — usually liked sandwiches, did they not?

She told me I would have to pay for any telephone calls I made, and she warned me that long-distance calls were not possible from this area; I would have to go to the *poste* in Pithiviers for that. Two baths a week were included in the price of the stay, but if I wanted more it would be extra. I opened my mouth slightly, surprised, and she half-closed her eyes in her shortsighted way, to see me better.

Was I ideal for what she had in mind? Looking back, if I try to see myself as she saw me at that moment, I suppose she might have thought I was. I was very young, after all. I was strong and healthy, despite my hardly awakened body. Perhaps she thought me innocent, probably because of my wide-spaced and clear gray eyes, the kind that are sometimes called candid in books.

She told me the village of Estouy was a fifteen-minute walk away; there was a big market in Pithiviers on weekends; there were wonderful castles within walking distance, bicycles to borrow, and if I wanted to go riding, Luis, the chauffeur, could drive me to the Fontainebleau forest for a small fee. She had loved to ride herself, once, she said and sighed, but she had been rather ill recently — and she fussed with the long sleeves of her gown and her hands fluttered nervously up to her neck. She mumbled something I did not quite understand about consulting several men of the medical profession.

She said that the young should enjoy themselves, and she laughed a little and leaned toward me and traced the outline of my cheek very lightly with the cool tips of her fingers as if to touch its youth. She said she wanted me so much to enjoy my summer with her.

I straightened my shoulders and pushed a stray lock of hair from my face as she had done. Vague, pleasant thoughts drifted through my mind: rides through leafy forests, visits to castles, dances in a white gown. Perhaps my sister had been right, after all, to send me here.

Madame sighed again and said youth lasted too short a time, and one should enjoy every moment of it. Somehow it sounded almost like a threat, and I felt the same sense of unease I had earlier. An expectant silence hung in the big, half-empty room. All we could hear was the sob of the water beneath the house.

I wanted to ask where her husband was. Had she grown tired of him? Or had my brother-in-law been mistaken when he had spoken of the baron's war record, his work in the Résistance? Had the man died young, as my father had? But all I could bring forth in French at that moment, awkwardly, was, "Do you have any children?"

Madame's light eyes turned dark and her hand fluttered up, dovelike, to the little cameo at her neck. But she covered my faux pas quickly. She laughed lightly, waved a hand dismissively, and said, "Just the dog, and, by the way, perhaps you would be good enough to walk him for me from time to time. I can see that he likes you already."

Madam assured me I could come to her if I were lonely, or I could ask for assistance from the cook or the chauffeur, Dolores and Luis, a Spanish couple, who lived in the cottage adjoining the mill and took care of the property.

Madame had become utterly dependent on them through the years, she maintained. Dolores did everything for her. She said the irony was that she, a French woman, could hardly boil an egg, whereas Dolores, who was Spanish — not a nationality noted for culinary skill — was a wizard. Luis was most serviceable; he was wonderful with flowers.

She waved her hand toward the window and told me that the garden had been laid out by a pupil of the great landscape gardener Lenôtre. Her family had been in the region since the time of Saint Louis. Of course, some of her ancestors had lost their heads here during the revolution, she added, and put her hand to the little cameo, a faded portrait she wore on a black ribbon around her neck. "Not all of the French aristocracy goes back that far, you know. There were all those so-called nobles created by Napoleon," and her mouth twisted into a slight sneer.

It was from the mouth that you could tell she was smart, savvy, she knew about people, about life. She described then, or perhaps at some later date, for my edification — it was a subject that came up frequently, I'm sure of that — all the different categories of French society: the *grande* and *petite noblesse;* the *haute* and *petite bourgeoisie;* the *Arabes,* whom I should watch out for as they were dangerous, ready with the knife; and the great undifferentiated mass of the *peuple.* I wondered in which category she believed I belonged.

I distinctly remember her saying, "Actually, do you know, the German aristocracy is the oldest in the world."

"No, I didn't know," I said, attempting to convey an interest in the matter.

She explained that she and her husband had had to sell off parcels of their land over the years. They had even had to give up the château before the war. It had recently changed hands again, sold to some wealthy Americans, whom I would meet. But they had kept the mill. "I have always thought it was very *cozy*," she said, using the English word with some relish. I looked in vain around the vast, half-empty room for any signs of coziness.

The mill was once even more remote than it was today. There was no bridge across the river. Until recently one had to take a pontoon to get to it, Madame informed me. Still, not many people came by. Madame peered at me now and said she hoped I would not find the summer *too* quiet. "But you look like a quiet one, not a nerve in your body, I bet."

I wanted to say my mother had called me "the radio" as a child, because I could never stop chattering, but Madame turned abruptly melancholy, and her eyes seemed a deeper blue. She said she could not say the same for her own nerves, fussing again with the sleeves of her gown, touching her hair. She added that she could not bear to be entirely alone in the house at night, and she was delighted to have someone so young and so charming here with her. Once again I wondered somewhat uneasily why this distinguished, married woman would need a young paying guest as company for her nights.

But before I could ask any more questions she rose to show me my room. A slippery back staircase led steeply to a small bedroom, the walls lined with green linen, peeling around the edges. The narrow bed, covered with a dark velvet counterpane and hard French bolster, pressed apologetically under the window. An armoire loomed against the other wall. Beneath one window a rickety table displayed a few yellowed magazines. The river, rolling softly like tears across a cheek, was the only sound. The room kept its secrets.

Beside it dusty stairs went up to a small and not very clean bathroom, equipped only with a *sabot* bath, where one was obliged to crouch, knees to chest. The enamel was stained blue-green under the taps. The small, airless WC was separate, as is often the case in French houses. Another door opened from the WC onto an attic.

Madame and I returned to what was to be my room and leaned against the low, creeper-covered windowsill, looking up at the glassy sky. A day moon shone palely in a delicate haze. The silver willows shimmered in the white light. The crows cawed. Madame turned toward me, her face sharp and white and slightly gleaming. Her eyes misted, and she blinked back tears. She placed her cool fingers, as light as pollen, on my bare arm. "It's the river," she said as though explaining her distress, her voice trembling.

There was a pause, a hush, and I glimpsed something, like the flash of a bird's belly suddenly gray, as it swoops down over water before rain. She mumbled words I could barely catch about a recurring nightmare, "the sort of dream that sticks to your skin, *vous savez?*" she said to me, her eyes glistening. I felt her fingers clinging to me.

"Oh, I would never leave you alone at night, Madame," I felt it necessary to assure her.

2

I HAVE LIVED in many places since that summer in the Loiret, but I still see the stone mill with all the vividness and the static, impossible quality of a dream. Because it was an unusually dry summer, the windows were often left open, on both sides of the house. In my memory they are always open, so that the sloping lawn, the white roses, the silver willows, and the river seem to flow through the house, as though there were no separation between inside and outside, between artifice and nature.

That afternoon, I took a walk with the dog in the high grasses that grew along the banks of the river, the cold water shimmering in the gloaming. The current moved slowly and in places was as clear as a reflection, and you could see to the gray bottom. On the river's banks two trees, a cherry and a willow, intertwined.

Then I settled into my room, putting away my few possessions in the big armoire, where they floated around. I should have brought more clothes, I thought. These were people who would dress for dinner.

From my window I watched Madame return in her

black Citroën. She had obviously been to the hairdresser; her hair was twisted up on her head in an elaborate chignon, two curls falling on either side of her face. She looked like a girl. Later, delicious scents emanated from her side of the house. Perhaps she was bathing or simply spraying on perfume.

I had already discovered there was very little hot water in that house or, in any case, on my side. The taps made a loud preliminary clanging, which promised great gushings of water but produced only a thin trickle of something brown, which, though initially scalding, soon became stone cold, if you can speak of water in that way. I washed, stepped out of the inch of brown water and into my black dress and my sister's tight high heels, and brushed my hair and tied it back from my face.

Madame, to my surprise, was wearing a narrow skirt with a slit at the back, which showed off her shapely legs in pink stockings, and a blouse of a pastel color, cut low to reveal her high, rounded breasts. The zipper of her skirt kept slipping down to reveal a shimmer of pink petticoat. Mother might have commented: "Mutton dressed up as lamb."

As we sat down for supper, there had still been no sign of the baron. My hostess sat with her back to the windows open on the long-stemmed daisies and beyond to the gravel courtyard and the dust path that led up the hill. The sunlight in the room was fading, but Madame had lit only the candles in the silver candlestick holders on the table. We sat in the muted light and ate in silence broken only by the scraping of the cutlery against the porcelain.

Madame had not lied about her cook. Dolores had slowly simmered pieces of tender beef in bouillon and red wine with new peas and tiny potatoes and shallots, adding mysterious herbs to the bouquet garni and other secret plants. She, who was indiscretion itself on every other subject, concealed their essence, so that any attempt one might make to reproduce her dishes was doomed.

My sister had told me, "And don't gobble down all the food, the way you usually do." But I had eaten very little breakfast before boarding the bus, and no lunch, so it was hard for me to resist. Madame picked at her plate in a distracted fashion, pushing the peas around.

From time to time she rose restlessly. Her foot tapped, her blue gaze roamed around the room and out the window; she lit up a cigarette, with her gold cigarette lighter, and then stubbed it out almost immediately; her little hands moved constantly, opening and shutting, fluttering up to touch her smooth hair, her perfectly made-up face, her cameo, her impeccable blouse, or resting for a moment, crossed like the wings of a pink butterfly on her heart. She hardly spoke, as though she were waiting for something to happen.

She must have noticed my gaze wandering over the painting above the mantelpiece, a copy of a Matisse, two purple sweet onions on a patterned plate. "Very sensuous, don't you think?" she asked me, moving her hands gracefully to convey her meaning. I nodded but wanted to tell her I had no idea what she meant. I had spent three months in Paris going diligently from gallery to gallery, staring at the paintings, unable to tell which ones I admired and seeing instead the flat dun fields and glassy blue sky and the white gables I had carried in my mind of my home in the Transvaal.

Then we heard the sound of a car descending the pathway, the wheels crunching the gravel of the forecourt, saw the high beams reflecting off the walls. Madame sprang up with remarkable celerity and lit the lamp on the mantelpiece. The room was suddenly so bright that the silver candlesticks were reflected in the dining table's cherrywood and the flames themselves dimmed in contrast.

In silence we listened to the car door slam, the fast footsteps, the plaintive cry of the front door. We heard a thud followed by swearing. He had forgotten to stoop and bumped his head on a beam. Madame put two fingers to her mouth, her lips curling. She whispered, "Always does that." Then Monsieur strode into the dining room, his keys still jingling in his hand.

He was tall and slender, well-proportioned, harmoniously built, and like Madame carried himself admirably, back straight, head held high. His face caught a sharp shadow from the lamp, and I noticed the features: high brow, straight nose almost pencil-thin at the tip, full-lipped but firm mouth. But it was the eyes, like Madame's, which struck me. They were very large and full of light and slightly hooded, as though the lids were heavy. Even at first sight, I was struck by his similarity to his wife. They looked like brother and sister.

His expression and his gestures, though, were different from hers. He had a distracted, impatient, almost angry air that evening, as though he were in a hurry to get through all of this and on to something better. He seemed impatient to dispense with the introduction to another paying guest. Madame said, "Here is our pretty little guest," and I blushed, but he hardly deigned to consider what she called my prettiness. He muttered, "Enchanted," but he looked anything but enchanted, appraising me with a cool, cursory glance. I felt it running through me like water.

Then, as though he had not found what he was looking for, he gazed into the distance as he shook my outstretched hand. He bent perfunctorily, lowered his head slightly in my direction, his fair hair catching the yellow light of the lamp. For a moment I smelled a heady mixture of cologne and smoke. My perceptions seemed suddenly sharpened. I saw the shine of the cutlery, the swell of the green lily-patterned curtains, the glint of the silver candlesticks.

He dropped my hand impatiently and moved away. I wondered if my contribution to the flagging family finances were worth the annoyance of my company. What if I were to do him the favor of slipping out the door and walking into the darkness? But where would I go? How would I pay for the months ahead, all my traveler's checks already used for this stay? The impossibility of leaving the place came to me then with all its dull weight.

I thought of Mother saying, "I want you girls to have the opportunities I never had." Learning a foreign language had seemed opportune to her. She had declared it was magical to speak another language, and the way to do it was to live in the country where it was spoken, and what could be more convenient on all accounts than for me to join my sister in Paris and help her during her confine-

SHEILA KOHLER / 22

ment? French was *the* foreign language to learn, the most refined, the one that would open the doors of art and fashion, good living, and pleasure.

I wondered how much opportunity to speak or even hear any language I would have with Monsieur. He did not kiss his wife or take her hand but sat down at the other end of the long table, like her masculine counterpart in silence. He studied the cuff of his gentian blue shirt and remarked how the new laundry he had found in Paris brought out its color so much more brilliantly than the one he had used before. Madame flinched at his words almost as if he had hit her or insulted her in some way. Her shoulders slumped, and she saddened visibly. They stared at one another in hostile silence. She put her fingers to her forehead as he did, as though she were his reflection.

Madame rang for Dolores to bring the rest of the stew in its big porcelain pot. This sparked Monsieur's interest, but when Dolores offered to serve me once again, my appetite had suddenly disappeared. Monsieur seemed pleased at my demurral, commenting on the high price of meat in France. When he had finished, the couple rose as though they had communicated by some secret sign and with identical words complained of fatigue and wished me a good night. I was left sitting at the table, alone.

I heard them ascend the stairs, speaking in the same soft, melodious tone, his voice slightly lower than hers, the same chord in a different octave.

The master bedroom was directly above the dining room. The walls of that old house were remarkably thin. Voices passed from room to room. As I sipped a cup of sweet coffee with milk, I heard light, rapid steps go back and forth. I imagined Monsieur lying on his back in the bed smoking impatiently, while she paced delicately before him, her porcelain-heeled slippers clicking and sucking, her little hands fluttering up and down all the while.

Then there was nothing for me to do but retire to bed with a book. The bedside lamp cast a dim light. The thick, rough sheets smelled of mothballs. A warm wind blew. A shutter banged. I dropped my book on the bare floor, threw off the uncomfortable bolster and the worn counterpane, and listened to the murmur of the river meandering beneath me.

I kept thinking of Mother sponging my hot body down and then sitting on the chair by my bed and reading *Anna Karenina* to me when I had the measles and was not allowed to read. She kept saying, "Darling, I'll read anything else to you, but I cannot pronounce all these Russian names!"

I should never have come here at all, I thought, but now that I was here, how was I to leave? I had very little money, and besides, where would I go? I would have to make a plan, telephone Cecile in the morning, ask for her help. I tossed on the strange soft bed in the half dark. My thoughts went round and round on the same tracks like a loud locomotive. I thought of Richard's narrow bed, the one that had collapsed under us while he was demonstrating how easily he could take my virginity. I saw his broad face, the quick brown eyes, and the shiny blue raincoat and matching beret he wore when it rained.

It always rained in Paris, it had seemed to me. At first I

had thought the fine drizzle would have no effect, not bothering to take a raincoat, hugging the walls as I walked, shivering. I sat close by Richard's side in a café, my shoes damp, listening to the rain fall softly outside. He was quoting a poem by Baudelaire. *"Mon enfant, ma soeur, Songe à la douceur d'aller là-bas vivre ensemble!"* he had said, leaning toward me. It made me think of the lemon tree in the sunlight in the patio outside the dining room at home. He put his arm around me, and I leaned against him and felt his soft, warm body through the thin raincoat.

I tried not to think of what had happened to me. It all seemed inconceivable now, as though it had happened to someone else, but I could see the doctor's house, the photos of his children on the mantelpiece. I could still feel the cold of the steel stirrups against my feet.

Bile rose in my mouth. I was sinking into the soft bed as though it were quicksand. The walls of the room pressed in on me. I wanted to descend the stairs and walk in the fresh air, but I could hear footsteps downstairs. Someone was pacing back and forth. I smelled smoke. I heard the back stairs creak.

I rose and tried to lock my door but found there was no lock. Anyone could enter and find me lying like a prisoner in a cell, helplessly exposed in my pink boarding-school pajamas. I ascended the steps to the bathroom and locked myself in. I stared at my wild face in the dim mirror in the moonlight: the pale skin, the wide-spaced eyes, the long, reddish brown hair.

Impulsively I opened the door that led from the bathroom into the attic. I leaned against the whitewashed wall of the big, dusty room, which ran the length of the house. Dormer windows peered down into the garden and let in narrow beams of slanted moonlight. An ironing board tilted against a wall, and a rusty washing machine squatted, one-eyed and sinister, a line of clothes drying above it. Dust-covered boxes and trunks were stacked on top of one another. A dressmaker's dummy with a faded feathered hat askew on its head stood in a corner, its round face feature-less. An old French provincial box-bed lurked in the shad-ows at the far end. It looked like a great cupboard, with panels of carved wood forming its head and foot, and a velvet curtain forming its side. I parted the dust-caked cur-tain and climbed up inside it.

There was a bronze candle-shaped lamp on a ledge along the wall beside some old clothbound volumes, as if someone had once retreated there to read, but I lay motionless.

Then I slipped my bare feet beneath the velvet counter-pane and felt something. A crumpled dress lay at the bottom of the bed. I pulled it out and held it up to the moonlight. It was an old-fashioned, narrow cotton sun-dress with buttons down the front and wide shoulder straps, one of them torn. It would have belonged to an older child or a thin adolescent. Madame might have worn it as a girl. It would have fitted me. I lifted it to my face and breathed in its musty odor.

I turned on the lamp and took up an old book lying on the ledge. Several issues of a magazine called *La Semaine de Suzette* had been bound into one volume. The magazines contained illustrated novels for children or young adolescents. I paged through the volume. The text was dull. I understood enough to determine these were sentimental, moralistic tales, and my eyes were closing when I noticed something odd: writing in the margins and on the back pages, at the heads of chapters, and even in some of the space breaks. Someone, perhaps more than one person — the writing did not seem to be the same — had written in pencil wherever there was any white space. Someone besides me had found this text dull, and my predecessors had even provided some of their own.

Two names were written out, sometimes as Anna and Lea, and sometimes entwined, as Annalea or Leanna, or even Liane, and they were decorated with flowers and small leaves and clinging tendrils and vines or sometimes even little smiling faces in the *a*'s. Some of the writing was so faded as to be illegible, but some, written in a clear neat hand, I could still make out. There was a date on one of the pages: August 1942, which was the year I was born. On one of the back pages I found a sort of cartoon of a slim, dark-haired man with a mustache. I thought I recognized Luis, the chauffeur. I did not fully comprehend the words I glanced at, but as I read them my head began to ache, the nausea I had felt earlier increased, and my breath came in quick pants. I was trembling slightly as I shut the book and closed my eyes, but some of the images remained with me even as I tried to forget them: children who never smiled, mothers beating their heads against the ground. Later, I was to return to certain of these words, and they would come to me with new understanding. That one sentence, however, stayed with me immediately because it was frightening.

Mother said everything would be all right; nothing seriously wrong can happen in France: is it not the country of the Rights of Man?

I fell asleep and dreamt. It is still a dream I dream at times: I am swimming breathlessly in flickering light underwater, descending toward the silt at the bottom of a riverbed. I swim around, catching glimpses of a child through the furry weeds and the fragmented moonlight. I try to swim away, but she comes fast toward me, as though inbued with some great strength. She throws her little arms tightly around my neck. They are unnaturally strong, like the clinging tentacles of some sea creature. I am increasingly breathless, fighting to free myself, struggling to unclasp those soft, dimpled arms, to reach the surface of the water, but the child clings to me desperately, her long hair blinding me, wafted by the water. Her face comes to me distorted, bloated, her skin gray-green and mossy, as though she has been in the water a long time. Her mouth is open wide in a frantic, soundless cry. I am struggling to reach the surface, but the child clings tighter and tighter, dragging me down and down. I bite hard into her neck, the blood curling in filaments through the water, staining it a deep pink.

I awoke in the moonlight, sweating and gasping for breath. Someone was, indeed, beside me. A face was close to my face, and I felt the labored, heavy breath. Someone had followed me up the stairs to the attic and thrown open the bed curtain. The sound of the footsteps on the stairs or the creak of the floor or the rings on the brass rod had woken me. I was filled with all the fear of a small child shut up alone in a dark space, unable to move or even to cry out.

For a long moment I was not sure where I was or who was leaning over me, or even if it were a man or a woman. The lips glistened as though rouged, the hooded eyes stared down at me with fear that mirrored my own. Then he said harshly, "What the hell are you doing up here!" It was Monsieur.

3

As I watch the sun rising across the park behind the tall gray buildings of this metropolis, I recall sitting at the table before the window in that room in the Loiret, the dawn light muted and pink. I was writing a letter to Mother, pressing down hard with my blue fountain pen, my hand shaking. I had hardly slept all night.

Afterwards I thought that my mistake was writing such a long letter to Mother recounting my woes. Like Candide, she preferred to believe that all was for the best in the best of worlds. She read only those thin romance novels, where it does not take much meandering before the heroine, who has lost her fortune and her heart, kisses the wealthy but misguided hero and lives happily ever after. She would read the same ones over and over, not realizing or perhaps not caring that she had already read them.

Later, I imagined Mother never read very far beyond the first few lines of my letter. She would not have wanted to know that I had met Richard on a bus, how I might have been ignored on the floor of a Parisian bus had he not rescued me. No one else had paid much attention to me at the time. Parisians seemed terribly bored by everything, even a young foreigner fainting inconveniently on a bus in the early morning because she had not eaten any breakfast. Nor, certainly, would she have wanted to find out how I had fainted once again, this time for good reason, at dinner while bringing in the roast for my sister, Cecile, and her husband, Jean Luc, and spilling a bottle of his good wine in the process. He was more worried about his wine than about his sister-in-law's fainting, it seemed to me.

Mother would surely not have wanted to be told how I had lain in my little blue room on the top floor of Cecile's house with its wicker furniture and the photo of a white magnolia and turned my face to the wall and wept and listened to the sound of the rain and felt the blood flowing from my body because of the intervention I had undergone.

How it rained and rained! How I stayed there, for what seemed like a long time or anyway until Cecile and Jean Luc thought it would be good for me to get out of my bed, that I was not sick, after all, and Jean Luc thought I should find somewhere else to stay for the summer. Mother would surely not have wanted to hear about this strange French couple who were now my hosts, about Madame de C, who seemed so fragile, and her husband, who seemed so impatient.

Then I decided it probably had nothing to do with my letter. Mother usually did as she wished, after all. She was used to getting her way and had been getting it ever since she was a young girl, even before she married my father, who had made and then left her a fortune. She was able to make her entourage jump by threatening to change her will.

I did not know how Mother would respond to my report. I knew she preferred to receive postcards of the having-a-wonderful-time variety, to which she would respond with a check. I thought she might wire, "Sorry you are having such a hard time. This for extra bath. Have fun." But she had other plans in mind.

The evening before I left for Pithiviers, Cecile and I had sat on the piano stool with her boy between us, his fat legs dangling back and forth, beating time. We were playing duets on the baby grand as we had done as children. The reflection of a silver jug of yellow roses shimmered in the surface of the piano. The photo of my sister and me, her arm around my shoulder, a petunia in her hand, glinted under the lamp. She was playing the melody liltingly in the treble clef, while I struggled with the bass chords. Her placid face was caught in a profile like a cameo in the circle of amber light, her plump lips open, her stomach swelling gently beneath her air blue dress, her curls clinging to her forehead.

Now, two days later, the sky still a pale pink, I was telephoning her, and awakening her at that. She mumbled, "Is something wrong, Dodo?" My sister, unable to pronounce Deidre as a little girl, had always called me Dodo.

"Yes, it is. I cannot possibly stay here."

"Why not?" she asked sleepily. I could hear Jean Luc groan in the background. I imagined my sister, propped up on white laced pillows, her eyes half shut. She had inherited Mother's creamy skin, her lucent eyes, her dark hair. Like Mother she had the rounded arms, the dimples, the sort of abandon that enabled one to enjoy what are usually called the good things of life: food, flowers, clothes. They were happiest shopping.

I told Cecile what had happened the night before, Madame's nervousness, the baron's brusqueness and un-approachability, my fright in the attic. She told me to hold on. I heard the muffled murmur of voices. Then she passed the receiver to Jean Luc. He cleared his throat. He was preparing a speech. Jean Luc made speeches on any occasion and on any topic and with great authority. He would, no doubt, be rushing off to make speeches to his women patients, of whom he had many, as soon as he had finished the one to me.

He began by explaining that it would be extremely annoy-ing to find one's paying guest roaming around one's home to places that had not been shown to her. He would proba-bly have sent the offending party packing immediately. One — the only pronouns Jean Luc used were *one* and *I* — must realize that French families, particularly aristocratic French families, were naturally very protective of their pri-vacy, that it would be considered extremely ill-mannered to go wandering around someone else's house in the middle of the night, reading books that did not belong to one, and sleeping in others' beds. Jean Luc pointed out that the de C's were a fine, old French family, that he had a memoir of one of their ancestors, a *maréchal,* and had seen the name mentioned in *Le Figaro* on several occasions. The baron — Jean Luc liked to say "the baron" — was particularly distinguished. The baron had received the Légion d'Honneur, or the Croix de Guerre, or some considerable honor for bravery at the end of the Great War, and had later been active in the Résistance. The baroness, for her part, had been considered a great beauty in her youth; everyone had been in love with her.

Jean Luc added that he was only sorry for their sake that the de C's had to resort to taking in paying guests. He hoped that my gaffe would be excused. "Don't forget to keep your hands on the table at dinner and not to cut your salad with a knife," he concluded, and Cecile concurred.

I wondered why intelligent women echoed their pompous husbands' opinions as though they were oracles.

"It's just that I don't have a good feeling about these people . . . ," I trailed off. What more could I say, after all?

Then I climbed the stairs and thought again of Richard. Perhaps I should have called him instead of Cecile. What would he say if I arrived on his doorstep? I had not spoken to him for weeks. He had not called me since Jean Luc had taken me to the doctor he had recommended, or if Richard had called, no one had told me about it. I sat down on the bed and counted the money I had left in my backpack. The dog had followed me upstairs. He sat by my bed, looking up at me with that doomed expression. I patted the bed in invitation, and he sprang up beside me with one bound. A terrible weariness came over me, and I lay back down, and we fell asleep, side by side.

I heard the sound of a voice: "Wake up, wake up. It's late. Time to get up," someone said, and for a moment, the gold light pouring into my eyes, I thought it was the light of the early mornings at home; I saw the flat fields stretching out, dun and endless. It was as if my arrival at the de C's had been only a dream.

Dolores dropped the tray with the half baguette with butter and the big bowl of café au lait across my knees like a bar and scolded the dog, who had jumped from the bed and slunk into a corner. Unasked, Dolores slumped down heavily on my feet, sighing, while I was forced to thank her and watch warily as she removed her flat slippers. I gathered she was preparing to remain, her weight tipping the narrow bed dangerously to one side.

"Eat up, eat up," she said, squinting darkly, addressing my mysterious double in her fractured French.

Sleepily I complied, wanting to question her about the bus and train schedules from this place, but before I could ask her anything she launched into a long description of her complicated and dramatic intestinal troubles. Her intestines were twisted or knotted, she maintained, resulting in a host of complaints: chronic indigestion and headache, severe stomach cramps. Then she moved from her intestines to her unhappy childhood, how she had almost died in a fire when her wicked stepmother had abandoned her in her crib to go to a bar with her lover; how she had been rescued miraculously by her father, who had had a vision as he was working in the factory, making shoes (was it shoes?) and had seen his house in flames and his baby trapped — such a beautiful baby she had been, with big black eyes, and soft black curls — in her crib, and how he had come running back through the crowded streets to find his house, indeed, in flames.

I waited for her to finish, feeling increasingly weighed down by her accented French words, like the wolf in the story whose body is cut open and filled with stones and sewn up again. It was difficult for me to interrupt, as I was still at the stage when I understood a great deal more than I could say. But I did eventually manage to ask her about the frequency of buses from here to Paris, still planning some sort of escape. She shrugged her shoulders and looked blank. She replied that she had never ventured farther than Fontainebleau herself, that Paris was a dangerous place, in her opinion, where one was as likely to have one's throat cut by an Arab as anything else. I must watch out, she warned, for the white slave traders who carried off unsuspecting young foreigners in dress shops when they were trying on dresses.

"Good heavens!" I exclaimed.

Then she rose to shut a window on one side of the room. She was terrified of drafts. Even in the summer Dolores wore flannel. She was always shutting windows, closing out the air, while Madame was always opening them.

I asked if Luis would post my letter for me, seizing the opportunity to shift the tray and get up before she could sit down on my bed once again, hoping to staunch the flow of her words. She had explained how Luis ferried the post back and forth daily from the post office in Pithiviers in the big black Citroën he drove for Madame. A slim, apparently spiritless fellow who wore a black suit with a tightly buttoned jacket, he had damp hands and a limp handshake, and sported a fine mustache and thick, dark hair, kept well-oiled as though, like Samson's, his strength resided in it.

When I think of the couple now, Dolores and Luis, they remind me of the nursery rhyme: Jack Sprat, thin and silent, sitting in his tight, dark suit opposite his fat, garrulous wife with her voluminous skirts at the narrow wooden table with the empty dish between them.

I perched on the windowsill in my pajamas, looking longingly out at the dust path that led up the hill, but this did not deter Dolores. She managed to prop herself up beside me, her short, plump legs dangling, and continued in her broken French — despite her many years in France, Dolores had never managed the language, which made it easier for me to understand because all her verbs were in the infinitive. She leaned closer and lowered her voice to warn me that despite his many other good qualities, she could not recommend her husband's driving. Her garlic breath was on my cheek as she confided, in strict confidence, that he had wrecked a beautiful white Lancia with red leather seats in Italy. "No one was seriously hurt," she added; "Luis is a lucky man," indicating with a nod of her head toward the window, the whereabouts of this prize.

She need not have worried about being overheard. Luis, I could see, was out on the big red tractor, mowing the lawn pugnaciously, turning his head to stare down with concentration behind him, as though conducting a personal vendetta against each blade. The air was redolent with the smell of cut grass.

Dolores continued with her disclosures, though she

turned out in the end to be unlike the housekeeper in *Wuthering Heights*. "Her" Luis — Dolores always referred to him in the possessive form — was younger than she. I must not tell anyone: she had falsified her age on her passport so he would never know. Oh, he had his faults, of course, like all men; he was not a "big" man in any way, if I saw what she meant. He did not bother her too much with his *champignon* in the night, which was a relief; in fact he was very shy, and did not talk much at all. But she knew she could count on him. He was extremely loyal. She had better be able to count on him, she said, squinting at me. Hah! if she ever caught him being unfaithful to her she would kill him, she said, demonstrating her method with a wringing gesture. As her dark eye appeared to be squinting at me while she was twisting her hands, I was not certain it was not my neck she had in mind, as though I were bent on his immediate seduction.

"Poor Madame is not as lucky as I," she said with a dying fall, followed by a dramatic pause. Dolores's talents deserved a larger audience than I could muster.

This was to be the price of breakfast in bed, I presumed. I wondered if Madame took in paying guests simply to provide Dolores with an audience. For Dolores, as for her intestines, everything was connected.

I learned that Monsieur's current mistress was not yet nineteen. Apparently he liked them very young. "Fresh bread" was how Dolores put it to me, enjoying the drama of it all immensely, I could see. This one, a tall, pale girl with wheat-colored hair who came from Normandy, had a little scar at the edge of her mouth that Monsieur found irresistible. She worked at *Vogue,* not as a model but as some sort of secretary.

"How do you *know* all of this?" I asked.

"Madame tells me everything. We are like this," Dolores recounted proudly, putting two fingers in the air and crossing them to demonstrate. Monsieur's mistress had recently fallen ill, Dolores went on, lowering her voice to a dramatic whisper: a cancer, down there somewhere, she indicated. Whether it originated in the uterus, the neck of the uterus, or the vagina itself she was not certain, but Dolores was sure how the cancer had manifested itself. The girl had bled profusely; Monsieur had been distraught; Dolores had found signs of Monsieur's distraction sprayed across his sheets when she made the bed in the morning.

"Poor Madame adores Monsieur so much. She is in despair. She will do anything to keep him. Without him she cannot exist," Dolores said, dramatically waving her plump hands. Madame had known him forever; their families had arranged the marriage before they were born. They had been to schools of the same kind, the same *rallyes,* the same picnics. Madame had known no other man. Ah, it made her quite ill to think of it, Dolores said, wiping her oily cheek, obviously enjoying Madame's distress, my consternation, and the drama of it all. "Madame is like a mother to him," Dolores went on. "She was obliged to comfort Monsieur in his distress, to call her own doctor for this girl with the cancer." Dolores was even afraid that Madame, in her distress, might do some irreparable harm to herself. She had had to rescue Madame in such a situation before. Ah, the number of nights she had spent sleeping on the floor beside Madame's bed!

Dolores told me she was as devoted to Madame as Luis was to Monsieur. She had worked for her for many years. She kept Madame's house as though it were her own. Indeed, they were very similar in so many ways. People sometimes took them for sisters. They were the same age, she maintained.

I looked more closely at her puffy, donut-shaped face. Though her skin was smooth, she looked far older than Madame because of her embonpoint. She had been with Madame since before the Second World War, when the de C's were living in the château, she said and mumbled something darkly about the goings-on around here.

I cleared my throat, fearing another incipient discourse would interrupt the current one. "Surely Madame was outraged?" I interrupted. "Surely she did not take all of this without a complaint?"

"All of this and more, much more," Dolores replied and stared with horrid insistence at me with her squint eye.

4

WHILE MASSAGING MY TEMPLES with the tips of her trembling fingers, as if to drag my mind into her well of memory, Madame spoke to me of her life. My headache distorted the sound of her voice, which came to me like the clanging of bells as I lay with my hot head in her lap. Her little fingers fluttered over my temples as she complimented me on my skin: "What a lovely gold it has become. Quite lit up, my dear!"

A month had passed since my arrival. The wheat, which was short and green when I arrived, had sprung up and ripened in all the uninterrupted sunshine. That was a summer of unusual drought in the Loiret, of hot wind and heat and heavy Bordeaux, the blood red wine the de C's kept in the small, dark cellar opening off the caretaker's cottage. The dry wind blew hard on the flat wheat fields and turned the white sky a dangerous gray. Above the golden sea of wheat, clouds whipped across the vast sky, casting strange shadows. Thunder and false lightning at night brought no rain.

Now it was late afternoon. The twilight lingered. What I missed was the fast blaze of sunset, the sound of familiar trees.

The tips of Madame's fingers on my temples trembled slightly, and she sighed profoundly, and I felt that unpleasant feverish sensation, the pressure on the temples, the heaviness of the eyelids. I could smell the half-stagnant water, and I thought of leaving as I had done repeatedly.

We were by the river on a blue groundsheet. Dolores maintained that wet ground would give you rheumatism. Drafts would give you a cold or a stiff neck. If you ate a certain type of wild berry that grew on the hedges around there, your stomach would swell up and burst.

That morning, like most, I had tramped fluid and automatic across those wheat fields. Leaning into the wind, I had dawdled in the shade of the hawthorne hedges, flecked with white flowers, and let the dog follow some scent, his dark head and flapping ears appearing from time to time above the wheat. I had wandered up the road to the farmhouse to buy the milk and eggs and cheese, passing the logs piled high for winter fires. I had sauntered past the small château, lingering at the iron gate, watching the two black swans glide, elegant and sinister, across the dark water under the chestnut trees. I had stopped to listen to the high, frail tune the shepherd played to his flock on a reed pipe, and the sweet sound of the music had made me think, as it often did, of what I had lost, and I had remembered the sound of a baby crying down the hall at the clinic, the thin cedar trees that grew along the wall at the doctor's house.

My head had begun to throb. I had cooled my feet in the fast-evaporating water of the river and hunted for tiny shellfish in the slippery riverbed. The mud banks were gray and cracked, and I had found dead fish there.

What I remember more vividly than anything else is the river, the air redolent with its slow-seeping water, its sound blending with the books I read, with Madame's voice, the soft touch of her fingers. Even before I could see it, I could smell and hear the river on my return from these daily walks. I would slip into the shallow water, sink down into the depths, and lie at the bottom in the silence, letting the current flow around me, hiding me like a liquid cloak.

As I walked on, alone and lonely, I often had the impression of someone watching me. Some imaginary dark figure, rather like the witch I had feared hovering behind my left shoulder as a small child, seemed to be lurking behind the trees. I imagined I heard a voice in the song of the wind. In my young and overheated imagination, and with nothing better to occupy my mind, I thought I saw Richard or Luis or Monsieur, or even some mysterious stranger, spying on me. I half-expected Monsieur to crash through the trees in riding boots or to burst forth like Rodolphe on his horse and surprise me, his Emma, a blue veil over my face. I felt sure someone was peering through the branches at me, someone who would discover me, would discover my changing body: the tanning arms and lengthening legs in my short shorts, the thick, reddening hair that I tied in a high ponytail, the swelling breasts, which seemed to be floating up visibly beneath my tight, cotton shirt. Even the odors of my body had changed, I imagined, the dark secret places more pungent, inviting.

I had the impression of becoming someone else, altered by this strange place, which I wished both to leave and to remain in forever. I felt, speaking the new French words I had learned from Madame and from the books I read, not only as if I were transformed but as if I were seeing the world anew, softened, made more sensuous, through the prism of this seductive, illusive language.

Sometimes I paddled an old leaky canoe I had found in the garage down the river. Once, as I was portaging it along the banks around some small rapids, someone did discover me. An elderly woman in black with a scarf around her head came striding angrily through the trees toward me and shouted at me to get off her land. She screamed that she would call the gendarmes. Had I no sense in my head? What was I thinking, a child of my age, taking a canoe down the river? Did I not know that some children had once drowned here?

I idled along the dust paths and found the railway tracks in the long grass, tracks that stopped dead, going nowhere. I walked up the hill to the village of Estouy, going past the gray shack where the poor children lived. The children rushed out wildly when they heard me approach, and I gave them apples I had picked or *carambars,* the hard, thin toffees I bought in the general store, and their mother stood grinning in the road, showing her missing teeth, holding the switch behind her back. As soon as I had passed she screamed at them and beat their sturdy little legs with the switch.

Now Madame stopped massaging my temples and drew back to look me over. She complimented my figure: "How nicely you are filling out, child," she said.

The *boulanger* came every midday, honking the horn of his gray Deux Cheveaux in the driveway until Dolores ran out to greet him, grasping the two long loaves still warm from the oven to her considerable bosom, putting her head in the window and chatting with him. The butcher sold us meat twice a week from his truck, folding down the side and sticking his red face out like Punch with a great grin. Luis watered the vegetable garden daily, and the sweet wild raspberries and juicy gooseberries ripened quickly in the sun. We picked apples, which Dolores stuffed with raisins and nuts and honey and baked or stewed with cinnamon or made into compote.

In the afternoons Dolores would spread the sweet cakes and scones and the strawberry jam and a pot of strong tea on the blue groundsheet on the lawn. Madame would motion for me to sit down beside her and offer me cake. "Eat, child, go on, it will look better on you than on me. We need to fatten you up a little bit," she would say and feel my arm, or pat my leg, like the witch, I thought, in *Hansel and Gretel.* For whose supper? I wondered.

Now she resumed her description of her life. She often spoke of herself with unusual and fascinating frankness, commenting on how unexpected her life had been, how unprepared she had been for it all, how no one! no one! had warned her what was up ahead. She said she felt young in some ways and also unspeakably old, ancient. Sometimes she felt so tired, so tired, unable to drag herself through

the day and yet never tired enough to sleep! She had so little appetite, had to force herself to eat. She had so little desire to do anything at all. How hard it was to wake in the
mornings and find all of herself there once again: the arms,
the legs, the head, all of the body to be dragged forth
through the long day.

She had been married off to her husband at such a
young age, hardly out of the convent. He had been sent to
the Jesuits, and she to the Sacré-Coeur, where the nuns had
taught her nothing! nothing! my dear, but how to embroi-
der beautifully and how to read romances secretly and how
to sing the Magnificat with her eyes turned back in a sort of
ecstasy with the scent of incense and flowers in the air.

Madame's life, and particularly, I have to admit, the details of her distress, fascinated me. I loved to hear her confidences, though I was aware, even then, that there was
something very strange about a woman of her age and distinction confiding such things to a young foreigner. I knew
there was something wrong about her choosing me as her
confidante, but her words both titillated and embarrassed
me, and though I would try to guide her thoughts into
more conventional paths, I could not resist for long. I was
quite happy to listen, flattered and surprised as well as
shocked that she would confide her most intimate secrets,
or what seemed to be her most intimate secrets, in me.

My own mother did not go in for such confidences. Her
life was hidden behind the thick walls and the shadows
of her room, in the hours she spent sleeping, in her long
silences or inconsequential talk of diets and clothes and
relatives. My own mother's mind had always seemed out of

reach, closed, full of secrets, but this woman, a stranger, after all, was willing to talk with unheard of frankness about things no one else — not even my school friends or my sister — had ever talked with me about before. When I thought of my mother I could hear the curtain rings drawn across the rod; I could smell the indoor plants and talcum powder and sweat. I could smell the odor of alcohol on her breath.

Each day from my window, after breakfast, I watched Luis dance gravely across the courtyard to the car. On his return I would run to ask him if there were a letter for me from Mother. I continued to expect some response to my long letter sent on the first day in that house. He would shake his head apologetically and cluck his tongue with sympathy, saying, "Maybe tomorrow," as though it were his fault.

Luis appeared to me more dignified, perhaps better educated than his wife. He spoke better French, and he wore his tight black clothes even when he worked in the garden. He had a peculiar walk, stepping softly and delicately with a slight limp, as though he were not simply walking but learning some complicated step. He moved quietly about the house, appearing on occasion out of nowhere, as though he had been listening behind a door. In stiff silence, Luis would drive me into Pithiviers to borrow books from the library.

When I was not walking the dog, or listening to Madame, I was reading. I lay on the lawn after lunch by the river and bolted French books day after day, reading indiscriminately, voraciously, with an appetite close to anguish.

Books became my way out, the open door from my own unhappiness onto another life. My own life that summer sometimes seemed extraneous to me. I read Stendhal, Flaubert, even *Bouvard et Pécuchet* and much of Balzac, so that now as I sit looking across the park at the skyline from this quiet high-rise tower, and take up a French book, even a dry, hot book like Camus's *Stranger*, I seem to hear the cooling sound of the river running through the pages, as I could hear it from every room in that place.

"What a little bookworm you are! We will have to show you something more of life," Madame would say. Now she said, going on about her own life, by the river in the gloaming, "The irony is," her voice low with a little catch in the words, "that I was not really in love with my husband. He called me heartless, because I couldn't bring myself to say I loved him. I had been taught not to lie," she added. "But I wasn't in love with anyone except perhaps Sister Marie Thérèse, the young nun in the convent." Yet, she *had* wanted so to please him — that had always been a fault of hers, this trying to please. She had so wanted his good opinion. He was hurt, of course, but he never complained.

She said they had been such good friends, such *copains*. They never fought, would talk and talk, play childish games — invent operas, singing different parts. "Oh, we were such children! In those days young people were much more innocent than now, and they had so much more fun — I don't think people have much fun anymore," she said and looked down at me rather sadly.

"I'm sure you are right," I said, and felt my temples ache again in a way that distorted the sounds of the evening: the leaves whispering, the water running, the crickets sawing monotonously. I wondered why there was so little fun in my life. I was not good at having fun, and when I had tried, it had brought me pain and banishment. What was wrong with me, then? And if I couldn't enjoy myself at seventeen, what was to become of me?

They liked the same activities, she and Guy: to ride, dance, listen to old opera records, take long walks in the forest. He loved this countryside as much as she did. "We have always known this place: the fields of wheat, the hawthorne hedges, the lilac spotted with fat, furry bees. It all belonged to our families. We were what was called the landed poor; it was understood that we were not to mix with the local children; all we had was one another, our ancient names, our pride, a few doddery retainers, and nature." She fluttered her little ringed hand in the darkening air, a rainbow flash — gesturing toward the river, the sky, the trees.

She went on while I listened in a sort of troubled dream.

"I know that Guy will come to like you. You mustn't mind him if he seemed cross," she told me, stroking my cheek with the backs of her fingers. I lay very still, recalling how his light blue gaze had flowed through my eyes and into my veins like water. I wondered where he was now, and why he had never returned since my first evening, to visit Madame.

She told me he worked in real estate. I never found out much about his work, what he actually did, or whether it was only his own real estate, field after field, that he was obliged to sell.

She had had the oddest sense that she could feel what he felt, she confided. Sometimes, imagine! she told me, they dreamed the same dreams. She remembered one about a snake coming out of a brioche, and she crooked her finger and straightened it to show me how the snake had come up through the little hat of the brioche.

"Such a French dream!" I exclaimed, sitting up, feeling rather giddy looking at her bright face.

She replied, "Oh, yes, yes, indeed, we are both very French, through and through." Once, she was walking in the fields and she had heard his voice in the wind, like the bells calling her to mass, like Jeanne d'Arc listening to her voices. She had rushed home to find he had cut himself badly falling off a wall, blood all over his leg.

Guy had been mad about her. He was so passionate, so possessive, always questioning where she had been. Oh, he wouldn't let her out of his sight, though they had not been able to conceive a child for years and years.

She confided to me in a trembling voice that her husband had not been able to make love to her at first, though he was ever so desperately in love with her. Oh, he had tried and tried, grinding at her miserably with his narrow hips, both of them sweating, their skins sticking together — ah! the awful sound of flesh slapping and sucking like that! with the blinds drawn in the hot summer afternoons on their honeymoon in the south of France. She had wandered barefoot through the lavender fields, glad to be alone for a moment.

My head throbbed increasingly and distorted her words strangely. Why was the woman telling me all of this?

She had always felt it was her fault: she was missing something essential, some sort of warmth that would have drawn him out, made him able to. . . . She shook her head. She was unable to love him the way she should.

And yet, all that time he had been so faithful, she told me. He had never looked at another woman. She had not been able to respond to his passion then, though she could conceive passion dimly, but not for him. She had been raised by her old maiden aunts in their flowered hats and gloves and later all those prayers in that dimly lit chapel. All that had nothing to do with life. What she had needed from a man was a touch of cruelty, not all that passionate insistence, which just made her feel guilty. Had he been more indifferent, she would have been less so. Ah, she had got what she had wanted in the end, she added bitterly.

Then she straightened her back, moved away from me slightly, smoothed the folds of her full cream skirt. Everything had changed during the last war, she said. The war had been a difficult time for everyone. France's position was ambiguous. There was so little food, even in the countryside, but that would have been nothing. She had been all right until something terrible had happened. He had become very different, distant.

She had watched couples kissing in the street or on the screen and felt as if she had been cast out, left out of all the joy in life. She had grown desperate, wanting what she had never wanted before, dispossessed of what she had never possessed. It was as if she had fallen in love with Guy just when she had lost him.

My cheeks felt hot, my body heavy. I sat closer to Madame, putting my arms around my knees, clutching them to me and smiling at her. Her breast went on rising and falling in the twilight, her hands fluttering nervously. I thought of Dolores's words, the gossip she continued to feed me every morning with the *tartine beurrée* and the big bowl of café au lait. I had wanted to tell her that I had no desire to know what had gone on here so many years ago.

"The papers called it 'Israel in the Loiret!'" Dolores had muttered, shaking her head, her fat cheeks filling with air like balloons about to explode. "Mind you, I'm no racist, you know, but somehow it is true they always end up taking the best houses in town, amassing huge fortunes, collecting jewelry, you know what I mean?"

I stared at her blankly. I was not interested in politics. I had grown up in a house without newspapers or with newspapers that gave only the most insignificant of news: "Monkey snatches baby out of cradle" was enough excitement for my mother. I had gone to a school where our history lessons had stopped before the First World War.

"What they had to do to get them to give up their belongings! They hid everything they could in eiderdowns, pillows, sewed money into the seams of coats," she said, lowering her voice further and adding, "even in the most private places. Foreigners!"

At first I was not certain what her words recalled. Certain images floated through my mind, a sensation of déjà vu. Had something like this happened to me, had I read it somewhere, or had I dreamed it? At the time, only some of the words came back to me vaguely. Later, in the quiet of the afternoon when Madame was taking her nap or had gone into Pithiviers, I was to climb the stairs back into the attic and page through *La Semaine de Suzette*. I read the words again, their meaning coming to me vaguely through my faulty French, the faint pencil marks, and time.

Remember the Polish woman screaming on her stomach while they looked up her bum for diamonds.

And the ugly, fat one who hid the anemone brooch in her corset?

She was disgusting, with her fat bosoms spilling out all over the place.

Poor thing, lying on the floor, with the gendarme beating her.

I lay my aching head down in Madame's lap again and listened to her voice going on in the dark, mingling with the melancholy purl of the river, which came to me persistently like the hope for happiness.

I saw a woman rip a pair of earrings from another woman's ears.

We should have tried to fish some of that stuff out of the latrine. We could have sold it.

Ugh! Disgusting! With those big fat white worms crawling around.

All those rings and necklaces and bracelets floating around in the shit. All those feathers and dust and the little children screaming.

The poor mothers left their eiderdowns behind so that their children would not be cold, and now they have nothing. They even took away their pots and pans.

They won't need pots and pans.

Madame went on, "You will see. We get everything we want in life, but only when we no longer want it."

5

S HE SAID, "You have such a pretty body. We must teach you how to show it off." I was walking down the dusty back stairs, I recall. Two weeks had passed since our conversation by the river. I had, I believe, been Madame's guest for about a month and a half. "I have seen you in the bath," she explained and made a gesture in the air conveying what she would have called *forme*. She had once walked in when I was crouched in the *sabot* bath trying to wash in the shallow brown water. "At seventeen you dress like an old lady in those shapeless baggy trousers and shirts, and why black all the time, my dear, like a widow?" she went on, fingering my buttoned collar.

Madame, herself, seemed dressed in new clothes: a tight dark skirt and a pale silk blouse. Her blue eyes glittered, and she smelled of her strong, sweet perfume.

"What would you have me do?" I asked with a shrug. After all, my traveler's checks had been used to pay for my small room with its stained wall linen, the lumpy bed with a hard bolster, two cold baths a week, and the privilege of speaking French with the Baron and Baronne de C.

Mother had still not responded to my request for money. I had not even received a postcard from her. I believed I could only take her silence as a rebuke. I believed she, too, must have considered me in disgrace. It was hard for me to imagine that she, who loved to linger in warm water, sometimes twice a day, would not want her daughter to bathe more frequently than twice a week. Every morning I watched out for Luis's return with the mail, but I no longer bothered to run out to him.

Nor had I had any news from Cecile. She appeared to have forgotten my existence. Richard, I had not heard from for months. It seemed that the people I loved had forgotten me entirely, and the small amount of money I had remaining would not have paid even for my return bus ride to Paris.

From this distance in time and place it is perhaps hard to understand my helplessness in such a situation. Why did I not go into Pithiviers and telephone my mother and ask her to send me a ticket home? It was becoming increasingly clear to me, I believe, that I should not stay on in this place through the long summer months, yet I was unable to conceive of an alternative. Part of the problem was perhaps the language, which I still grasped only haltingly despite all my desperate reading and listening. I still felt partly like an idiot, half-realizing what was happening around me, unable, even if I understood the words, to comprehend the sense, the allusions, the references, the undercurrents. It was as if I were younger, rather than older, much younger than my years. I felt that I had lost my own family's approval, at least for a period of time, that there was nothing

I could do but wait out this banishment with these strangers.

This particular afternoon I remember having no desire to accompany Madame on the shopping expedition she proposed. I had always hated to shop: the crowded streets, the big stores, straggling behind Mother and my elder sister through racks of dull dresses. But Madame waved away my objection, shrugged her narrow shoulders, tapped with authority on the old marble floor with her very high heels, and pursed her glossy pink lips. She had a way of expressing her opinions with authority. She could be high-handed, mercurial, suddenly remote: she entered rooms without knocking, threw open windows; decided we were to take tea inside when the wind made her ears ache, what time we would dine, when I should not walk the dog, because it was going to rain, though it did not rain, day after day. She had me pour the tea, and when I had filled the cups and passed them and sat down again she would say, "Give the poor dog a saucer, too, won't you dear, I'm sure he must be thirsty." In her absence, the household seemed to lose its focus: Dolores and Luis would withdraw disconsolately into their cottage; I would drift indoors and out aimlessly with my book.

"No problem. Your credit is good," Madame said flatly now and took my hand and linked her arm with mine, her bracelets tinkling, her silk rustling, as she led me to her car. It was as though she were moving a pawn to the next square of a chessboard.

*   *   *

Luis drove us into the central square in Pithiviers. He was the most reckless driver I had ever encountered. I presumed Madame had taken him on as a chauffeur because of either his gardening — the white roses that grew in such profusion, with their transparent petals and odor of wine — or his wife's cooking, or their willingness to work for the modest wages she offered — the ever indiscreet Dolores had, among other things, complained about their salary. Her Luis drove as though driving were the only revenge for his submissiveness. In his hands the big black Citroën became a vehicle of death. He drove dangerously fast along the narrow, winding road. He drove too close to the car in front of him, slammed on the brakes suddenly, and passed recklessly.

As he turned on the engine, I felt the old Citroën rise slowly and descend as though we were traveling on water rather than solid earth. Madame and I sat in the back, pallid and trembling, terrified. She clutched my hand, made little sucking noises through her teeth, and slammed her small, elegantly shod foot onto an imaginary brake. Perhaps, it occurred to me, Luis was stirred to further recklessness by her distress.

On Saturday the Pithiviers market spread its stalls through all the main streets of the town. Vendors sold everything imaginable, from apple parers to underwear, in the dappled light and shade cast by the thick chestnut trees. Innumerable and delicious cheeses were displayed: soft Bries melted on straw mats; Reblochons ran into vine leaves; Saint Albrets ripened; and cylindrical, pyramidal, and log-shaped chèvres, cheddars, Muensters, and marbled Roqueforts perfumed the air delicately. Blanched celery roots, fat, tender artichokes, pale yellow endive, dark green spinach, pungent tomatoes, succulent pink-and-white peaches, and plums as dark as bruises were piled up on the wooden trestle tables.

The butcher who came to the house twice a week parked his gray van in the main square in the shade of a poplar. Grinning widely, he leaned out of the side of the van in his bloodstained apron and checked smock, with all his meats displayed: skinned rabbits and tender steaks hung from iron hooks; small, still recognizable lambs and half-plucked chickens lay helplessly on the counter, their heads folded back under their wings, clots of blood like rubies in their beaks.

This time, Madame and I were not buying from the stalls. We strolled lazily in warm sunshine, arm in arm. We sat in the main square under the awning of a pastry shop. The pink of the awning made Madame's pale face look rosy. She ordered herself a *menthe verte,* and me a *mille-feuilles.* She continued her fascinating disclosures, speaking of her childhood, her marriage, fluttering her hands, little pink wings in the air. Her eyes often glittered with tears as she spoke, and her voice caught with emotion.

She confessed that sometimes she had felt, looking at a woman, what she should have reserved for a man. There were certain kinds of young women who appealed to her: something in the skin like the phosphorescent light that moves of itself on the night surface of southern seas, or perhaps her need to protect someone younger, more vul-

nerable. It was just for a moment, of course, and naturally
nothing had ever come of it, but even so she had to admit
that she had felt, staring into the depths of some young
woman's eyes, something warm, something joyous, as if
she could reach out and grasp life itself.

The tips of the trembling chestnut leaves were touched
with gold, as though the boundaries had dissolved, and I
remember thinking solemnly — the girl of seventeen that
I was then: *This woman has shared something profoundly intimate with me.* I imagined corridors in her mind were leading into secret chambers, cool, shadowy, shuttered rooms
where no one else had entered and to which she was ushering me and throwing open the casements on the sunlight.

She spoke of the balls she had attended, her early con-
quests, so many of them, all the hearts she had broken.
Now, in this marriage, her own heart had been broken and
broken again by her wayward man, she said, her eyes glittering, her wide mouth trembling.

I wanted to say how much I admired the determined and
courageous way Madame faced adversity, keeping herself
up so beautifully, running her household so smoothly: all the
silver shining, each object in its place, the flowers in vases,
the lawns smooth, the roses pruned. I thought of my own
mother, who had moved from the big house when my father
had died and had then gone from one flat to a smaller one
and finally into one room in a hotel, packing us off to boarding school. I wanted to confide that she was far too good for
him, that she was wasting her life on him, but all I could do
was reach out and grasp her small, pink hand. She held on to
me tightly and shook her head and confessed she was so glad

that I had decided to spend the summer with them, that my young presence had filled a great emptiness in her life.

Then she looked around the square, with its stone monument to the war dead and its garish circle of red and orange and purple flowers, and sighed deeply and said she had been coming here every summer now for more than thirty years. "Even during the war," she said and glanced about her distractedly.

I said, "Yes, Dolores told me about what happened here during the war."

"She would do better to keep her maw shut on *that* subject," Madame said suddenly with asperity and withdrew her fingers. I had always known that harsh tone was there under the sweetness of her voice, but I had never heard it so clearly before. She turned her head and looked at me shrewdly from the side of her light eyes. "What *did* Dolores have to say?" she asked.

I shrugged and shook my head vaguely and said, licking up the remains of my pastry from the side of my fork, "I wasn't really paying much attention. She says so much about everything. I think it was something about certain people being better behind bars, rather than owning all the best houses in town. Was she talking about the Jews?"

Madame drew herself up and shook her head. "Taking advantage of helpless people, coming back with gold earrings and wedding rings in their pockets," she muttered. She looked at me as though she were considering something. She leaned toward me and said, lowering her voice, "I am going to tell you what really happened here during the war, before someone else gives you any more false information."

I waited for her to continue.

"There was nothing we could do. These people were refugees, after all, mostly Poles and Germans and a few Dutch; the ones from Germany behaved better than the rest, actually. We simply sent them back to their homes."

"They were deported?" I asked and thought of the words from the margins of *La Semaine de Suzette,* to which I had returned occasionally with nothing better to do in my dull afternoons.

> *What does "deported" mean?*
> *Sent back to your homeland.*
> *And France, then? What is France?*

For a moment my lips parted and I was on the point of asking about the books in the attic, but something restrained me, and also, Madame was still speaking, as if she were reading from a book herself. It was not the sort of tone one could interrupt. "Besides, no one, surely, and least of all the Jews themselves, could imagine what their fate would ultimately be. No one, no one, in the summer of '42 knew about the gas chambers!" Madame almost shouted at me, her face very red. "But I have no wish to say anything else."

"Naturally," I said with relief. "There are so many more interesting things to talk about."

But I could not help but remember what I had read.

> *I felt I was watching a movie, in slow motion, and it was happening to someone else: climbing up into the cattle car with Maman, the policemen pushing and hitting, demanding that we climb faster.*

Adults being beaten! How can an adult be beaten?

The German soldiers with the red stripes on their trousers striding toward us, making us get off the train and go back to the camp. Why did they separate us from Maman? How could they do that?

Because they said we were too young. Only the older ones went. Because we were the lucky ones.

How can you say that! I would rather be with Maman, wherever she went. Even dying, I would be less afraid if we were together.

Madame wiped her lips daintily with her linen napkin, patted my hand benevolently, and regained her composure. "What fun," she said, and a smile flickered briefly across her face, lighting it up once again. Instantly, like a girl of my own age, she was full of gaiety. A mood of revelry seemed to have taken hold of her, and I wondered if Monsieur were about to pay us the compliment of a visit.

Every time I hear footsteps on the stairs I think they are coming for us. I wish Maman were here. I keep seeing Maman standing there, while they pulled us away from her. I want Maman.

I want to live! I want to live!

Then she was leading me through the new door in an ancient building on the corner of the street opposite the church. Bells were ringing as we entered the softly lighted interior with its pink carpet and papered walls and small sofa and chairs.

At first I was not sure where we were. There was no sign of clothes except for a few items draped discreetly, almost apologetically, in the corners. An elderly woman in a black dress with a white collar, who looked more like a head-mistress than a saleswoman, immediately greeted Madame effusively. She was a tall, severe-looking woman, and the only mark of her calling was the little pincushion filled with gold-tipped pins on one of her gaunt wrists. "Madame la Baronne," she rhapsodized, clasping her hands together fervently.

Madame said she wanted to see something pretty for this pretty girl. The saleswoman stared at me, tilted her head, and then seemed to melt as she smiled down at me, as though she had found a long-lost child. She installed us on the plush sofa with its numerous plump cushions and offered us coffee and cream in thin porcelain cups, sugar in different colors, and a small dish of *petits beurres*. She sat opposite us on the edge of her seat, one bony elbow on her knee. She leaned confidentially toward me and asked discreet questions in a low voice about my taste and occupations. Then she brought out the clothes, item by item, opening each cupboard and closing it quickly behind her, as though reluctant to expose her secrets.

Clothes were my sister's and Mother's domain. I had left the chore of buying my clothes up to them when it was strictly necessary, and had been content to wear an old pair of dirty blue jeans when I was not in my school uniform. But sitting close beside Madame, the air redolent with her perfume, sipping the little white cup of sweet coffee and cream and nibbling on a *petit beurre,* in the muted pink light of that seductive room, I was drawn irresistibly into this ancient ritual. I watched as Madame cleared and then donned her glasses for this important work. She carefully considered every item. She felt the material between finger and thumb, surveyed the cut, checked for deep seams and hems, for linings, hand stitching around the collars. She used her hands eloquently to show me the advantages and disadvantages. She convinced me to try on one outfit after another.

So I paraded before her as she sat on the sofa or rose to get a closer look. She tapped around me in her high heels, and the saleswoman followed behind her like a tall priestess, carrying her offering, her pins. Madame praised my figure, my face, my coloring, the way I walked, tactfully hinting at some slight alterations in my bearing. "Of course, everything looks good on her, particularly when she holds her head high and her *petit popo* in" — this said with a little pat on my behind — "yes, yes, that little shelf you young girls have down there," she added, longing in her voice. They tilted their heads and smiled, gazing at me mistily. They reached out their hands to adjust a pleat, shake out a fold, or shift a shoulder pad, or simply to touch my face, as though I were a source of heat and they, two inhabitants of some cold region.

Walking back and forth between mirrors in one new outfit after another, holding my head higher and higher, thrusting my pelvis forward and swinging my hips, I gradually began to see the reflection of someone else, a pretty, sexy, reckless creature, who knew how to walk, how to hold herself erect, how to swing her hips voluptuously, how to enjoy herself, how to live.

I strutted before the two admiring women in bright tight pants, which showed off my ankles and some of my calves, and in clinging tops and low-cut blouses, which exposed my budding breasts.

"We must have that," Madame kept saying, throwing yet another outfit onto the chair with a flick of her wrist. "No, no, we've chosen quite enough," I replied, resisting feebly. All was put down to credit, Madame's credit, to be paid off at some vague future date.

It was growing dark outside. We had been in the shop for hours. The saleswoman had long since barred the door to other customers. I was enjoying myself too much to resist, stung by a fierce longing for pleasure, any pleasure.

Then came the white crepe evening dress with a tight waist and a low neck and a flared skirt. Madame said, "It's perfect," and her acolyte, pen poised to add the considerable sum to the bill, agreed.

"I will never wear it. When could I?" I protested.

I hate the way people looked at us in the street.
Disgusted, they looked disgusted.
We disgusted them because we were so dirty and badly dressed.

"You will wear it. We will have a party, for you."

"A party for me?"

"For your birthday," Madame added.

"How did you know it was to be my birthday?" I asked, amazed. Had Cecile telephoned? Would she perhaps surprise me at this party? I saw her face, her slanted smile, the dark curls around her forehead, the rounded arms.

"Ah, a secret. It was going to be a surprise, but now you will know. Is there anyone you would like to ask?" Madame inquired.

I thought of Richard, remembered the six flights of stairs on the Rue du Cherche-Midi that led up to his narrow room with its balcony, his dark socks hanging on the railing to dry. I recalled the odor of fried potatoes. What would Madame say if I invited him? And he, would he come? Why had he never contacted me? Would he want to be with these people? No, he wouldn't. He would not feel at ease with them. He would consider them snobbish, superficial, strange. He had probably forgotten all about me by now.

"There is no one I know, here," I said and hung my head.

"Never mind," Madame said and promised to invite the guests herself. She ticked them off on her ringed fingers. She would have the de La Tour d'Auvergnes — the pinkie — such a charming couple, cousins of the Giscard d'Estaings, did I know? and the de la Valliéres — the ring finger — the husband was in the Senate, and her old friend Sophie de Montesquieu, such a distinguished family — the middle — and she supposed she would have to ask the Americans — the pointing finger, she could never remember their names, something odd — 'Awthorne or something like that — they had so many of those millions, my dear.

Madame went on. She would make sure that her husband would be with us that night. I can still hear her saying, her voice dipping and trembling slightly with emotion, "Ah, wait until Guy sees you in this dress!" gazing at me and pressing her hands together to form a pyramid and lifting them to her lips, as though she were praying.

By then, I would have bought anything Madame wanted me to buy. I would have done anything she wanted me to do. I emerged from the shop into the square in a full, soft skirt, which blew against my legs, and a low-cut top in a bright pink. I felt flushed and dizzy and in love with Madame, with Monsieur, the whole world.

Luis brought the car up, and Madame climbed in the back. He placed the pink packages carefully on the seat beside her. Then he opened the front door and inclined his head, his glossy hair falling forward, putting his damp palm under my elbow to help me into the car, as though I were suddenly infirm.

He took off with a sickening lurch and drove even faster than usual, turning his head constantly to stare at me. "Beautiful," he hissed, embarrassing me. I turned my head to Madame, most probably just to stare at her, but she, as though the whole business had worn her out unduly, or perhaps because she preferred oblivion to Luis's driving, had promptly fallen asleep in the back of the gray leather interior of the Citroën, a tiny driblet of saliva, like a pearl, in the corner of her mouth.

I concentrated on the narrow road, lit up by the headlights, as though, by example, I could convince Luis to do likewise. But he turned his head again to survey me, his gaze lingering dangerously. I took advantage of the situation to ask, once again, if there were anything from home for me.

"Nothing for *you*," he said and looked at me, with what I took for a faint gleam of hope in his dark, long-lashed gaze. He swung one arm across the back of the seat. He looked into the mirror to stare at Madame, and the car lurched dangerously across the road. "Watch out!" I warned. He leaned toward me and added in a low voice that he could tell me something about Madame that might interest me, if I would like to know it. I drew myself up and glared at him, thinking that he was angling for my newfound charms. And was he? He was not. He was not.

I told him that I had heard enough gossip about the de C's from his wife, thank you very much.

He muttered dramatically and solemnly, "Dolores does not know all," and grasped the wheel with two hands. I told him she knew more than enough for me, and he turned his gaze, for once, to the road.

In the dimly lit hall, Madame sighed and said she was exhausted, she was going to sink immediately into a bath, and why did I not do the same? "I've already used up all my baths for this week," I said.

She shrugged and said, "No need to hold back. Go ahead and take as many as you wish from now on."

"You're so generous to me," I said and went to kiss her on her cheek, but Madame put her hands out to stop me. We stood facing one another in silence. All I heard was the hum of the river gliding under the mill. Madame stood very erect beneath the low-beamed ceiling with her trembling hands on my shoulders and gazed at me as though there were something she wanted to tell me but not right then. She whispered in my ear, "You must not expect too much of people, dear, then you will never be disappointed. Human beings are not gifted at happiness, you know. Most of us are much frailer than we seem. Never trust anyone completely, not even me."

6

"YOU ONLY TURN EIGHTEEN once in your life," she said, and declared she would run my bath. It was my birthday, several weeks since our visit to Pithiviers. Only certain moments from that summer have remained clearly in my mind, and long periods passed without memories of any kind. That evening I remember vividly. I was to bathe in Madame's big bathroom. My hostess told me to bring whatever I might need, and she led me up the front staircase. As she climbed quickly her high-heeled slippers rapped and her bracelets jangled. She turned the metal taps on all the way, and the water rushed in generously, steam rising. She leaned over the bath and drew the curtains, with their faded pattern of pink primroses. She poured lavender bath salts that fell like ashes into the water, and hung my white dress on the bathroom door, so the steam would smooth the creases from the full skirt.

"Well, get in," she said as I hesitated, huddled in my toweling gown, clutching the blue plastic soap dish I still had from boarding school. "Go on, enjoy yourself," she insisted. I stared at her, glanced at the door, folded my arms over my chest, and clutched my armpits protectively. "You Anglo-Saxons are all such prudes at heart. Do you think you have anything I haven't seen before?" she added.

Still, as soon as I had let the gown fall and slipped into the full, warm bath, she turned to stare. She sat down on the bathroom stool with its frilled skirt and gaped at me, her mouth slightly open, perspiration beading her upper lip. For me there was no turning back. I ignored her, put my head back, shut my eyes, and stretched out languidly.

I had spent all day lounging on her lawn. The wind had stirred the pages of my book and shaken the silver leaves, which shimmered in the white light, and the water had flowed on between its slippery banks, murmuring as it passed over the moss-covered stones. I had waited in vain for something from Mother or my sister for my birthday. Had they both forgotten me entirely? My pocket money had almost entirely run out. This, I had begun to realize, was to be a summer of tramping across those flat French fields with Madame's dog for company. She alone was offering to celebrate this day.

"Here, take this," she said, leaning over to hand me a new cake of Guerlain soap. The wide sleeve of her silk gown fell away from her arm and dipped into the water. "We want you to smell extra sweet tonight."

I lay there flushed and drowsy with the warmth and the steam and the familiar fragrance of lavender. She stirred her hand in the warm water. "Guy will be as pleased as I am with how you have changed," she said and rubbed her finger over the fine lines around her full mouth. I wanted to tell her it might be better for us both if her husband never came back. Her smile flickered briefly, lighting up her eyes. She added, laughing over her shoulder as she left the room, "And make sure you wash the essentials, dear."

When I emerged from the bathroom, wrapped in the towel she had put over the warming pipes, her bedroom door was ajar and I could see her from the landing, as she sat on her dressing-table stool brushing her fine hair with a silver-backed brush, the quick strokes setting off little points of light like stars in her hair.

Her bedroom windows were thrown open onto the smooth lawn and the river. At this evening hour the mist lay in the valley, and the sky had turned a pale violet. The house was filled with the smell of freshly cut grass.

"Come in, come in," she called melodiously. I had never been in her bedroom before, and I stood in the doorway and looked at the cream silk counterpane on the wide bed, and the old porcelain doll in its ruffled bonnet and flounced skirt, propped up on white lace pillows. She picked it up and showed it to me, lifting its skirt to expose its pantaloons and petticoats and the embroidered bodice. She told me the doll's name was Marie Antoinette, that it still had its original clothes, and that she had had it since she was a child. She was beautiful but reputed to bring bad luck.

"And now come here and let me make you up. You won't do it well," she said and took my dress and underthings and lay them out on the counterpane, led me over to the dressing table, and placed me on the stool, with its organdy skirt over green silk. The kidney-shaped, glass-topped table held her silver brush and comb set, her unguents and rouges and powders in porcelain and cut-glass pots with silver tops.

She pulled the towel firmly down to expose my shoulders and breasts, pink from the hot water. Her hands trembled as she lay them on my shoulders. I leaned toward her and felt the warmth of her body against my back.

"Everything is under control," Madame said with conviction. She sat down beside me and set to work with energy and expertise: she smoothed makeup, rouged my cheeks, the lobes of my ears, and the tip of my nose. She outlined my eyes.

I sat before the mirror and listened as Madame explained how to soften the green eyeliner by blurring the outlines. "Everything must be veiled, *fudged.*" She smoothed the green away from my eyes, coloring my eyelids with firm strokes while I watched my gray eyes turn blue. "See, they look blue now, like mine," Madame said. She coated my lashes with so much heavy mascara that I could hardly open them. When I lifted my hand blindly to help, she tapped it smartly. *"Reste tranquille!"* she said.

I stared at myself in the mirror. My small gray eyes looked suddenly large and somber, and the white-tipped lashes, thickened with mascara, gave my gaze a shadowy, secret quality. My mouth, painted a glossy pink, looked fuller and harder, as though I knew about people, about life. My lips looked heavy and ripe, like fruit about to fall.

Madame had made me up to look like her. We might have been sisters. She noticed the resemblance. She put her hands on my shoulders and said, "You, too, have known disappointment. That's why you understand me so well."

She opened her armoire, poured out two glasses of something amber, and brought one over to me, the sticky liquid dripping down the sides. "Here. It will give you courage," she said.

I threw back my head and drained the glass. The sweet, strong alcohol supplied me with a new warmth. I licked the remains greedily from the side of the glass.

She told me to slip on my underthings and to fetch my dress. She pulled it over my head, plunging me into the airless dark for a moment, as though I had dived into deep water. She fumbled with a hook, which had caught at the neck. When I came up for breath, gasping, she made me stand very straight before the mirror and told me to draw in as she pulled tightly on the blue silk sash.

She put her hands on my hips. "Lovely," she said and held me close. I could smell her sweet, strong perfume. She kissed me lightly, turning her lips as pink as mine. The whole world spun around me, the pale parquet floor, the sea green dressing-table skirt, the silver-topped pots, the lilac sky, Madame's eyes, all spinning.

"Now choose something for your neck." I looked down into the cluster of bright things: jeweled necklaces lay entwined and glistening like sleeping serpents. "But I couldn't. I might lose it, and have to work for the rest of my life like in the Maupassant story."

She laughed and said, "But these jewels, I'm telling you, are fake. The originals were sold years ago. And the rest have been given to me for one reason or another," and she put her cool fingers around my neck. I chose the cameo I had seen her wear on the first day I was there, the one I had somehow understood from the start had some significance. At first she protested, suggested something else, but finally she looked pensive and said, "Yes, wear that one. I'd like you to wear that," and tied the thick black velvet ribbon around my neck so tightly that I had to slip a finger underneath to let in some air.

"And now go downstairs and see if Monsieur has arrived. Entertain him, will you, dear, while I dress?" she urged.

That evening the rooms seemed bigger and emptier than ever with all the Louis Quinze furniture lined up expectantly against the walls. With the oilcloth covers removed, the egg yellow fabric appeared bright and new. The black-and-white marble floors glistened. Roses and dahlias and long-stemmed lilies fanned stiffly in glass bowls on the tables between the windows.

Dolores had polished the silver to a high shine, and Luis was busy setting up the bar in the music room, whose glass doors opened off the salon. He was busy mixing and shaking drinks and stirring in ice and throwing in cherries while humming Spanish dirges and ordering the musicians around imperiously. There was to be dancing after dinner. "For your eighteenth birthday, we must have dancing," Madame had said, and I had kissed her cool, smooth cheek.

When Luis saw me standing in the doorway to the music room, his eyes lingered on the cameo around my neck until they turned black. I put my hand up to cover it. Luis said, "You are wearing Madame's cameo."

"She lent it to me," I replied and turned away. There was no sign of Monsieur.

I helped put out the hors d'oeuvres Dolores had made: little quiches and pizzas and foie gras on toast, stuffed eggs, pâtés and olives on round silver trays. I shut up Madame's dog in my bedroom, where I could hear him howling miserably.

Then everyone was arriving at once, a great flood of laughing and chattering, and Dolores was rushing back and forth in her black dress and white cap and apron, ushering everyone inside, showing the men into the living room or the downstairs cloakroom, taking the women upstairs to Madame's bathroom to adjust their windswept hair or powder their noses or find a spare safety pin. Guests had driven from Paris in smart red sports cars with the tops down, or come from Pithiviers and the local towns in big dark sedans.

I moved among them stiffly, smiling. I swung my hips. I thought back to parties at home: the girls all blushing and giggling together in little clusters on the veranda, admiring one another's dresses and eyeing the boys and pulling their fringes over the pimples on their foreheads; the boys sweating in the garden, drinking nonalcoholic punch; and everyone happy to be on holiday from boarding schools, run in the tradition of English ones from the preceding century; and Mother, staggering down the steps blindly, drunk on her gin and tonics.

I knew none of these guests, and they all knew each other. They greeted one another gaily over my head, the women kissed, one, two, and three times (left cheek, right cheek, left cheek), linked arms, leaned close, and whispered in one another's ears. They were all slim, the way only French women can be. All of them had pointed, pretty-ugly faces and slender legs and tiny waists, except for the ancient Comtesse de Courtois, who was plump and friendly. She complimented me on my dress and said what a pity it was her son had not been able to attend the party, as she sprawled on a sofa in a corner, fanning herself and asking if I could possibly help her loosen her skirt.

The women wore silk dresses or suits with brightly colored blouses and pale stockings with the seams dead straight, and big diamond brooches in the shapes of moons or stars. Their hair was pinned up in elaborate chignons, or hung straight and silky around their narrow, intelligent faces, or cut to fall in an even line to their chiseled cheekbones. They held their heads high on long, slender necks and flashed perfectly manicured red nails, ignoring me.

"I hear they have a new one. They had some problems, I believe, with the one before," a woman in sapphire earrings said, lowering her voice.

"Can't think why they do it, really. Surely they're not that hard up?" an elderly lady in pearls replied in a whisper.

"Certainly, one wouldn't say so tonight," the sapphire earrings said, looking around the room with envy at the sparkling silver, the big bowls of flowers, the plates of expensive hors d'oeuvres.

The men were handsome and dapper, in well-tailored dark suits, with shirts in all the colors of the rainbow and gold, silver, or onyx cuff links and white foulards sprouting from their pockets like lilies. They looked me up and down brazenly and leaned too near when they wished me a happy birthday, using the occasion to plant a wet kiss, to put a hand on my waist or my buttocks, crushing my dress and my breasts as they drew me firmly against their bodies, and whispered lewd, teasing remarks hoarsely in my ear.

Conversations swirled and eddied around me, floating fast, rolling onward, like the river beneath the house. They went from politics — de Gaulle, the Algerian question, and the use of torture — to Camus and a new play by Sartre called *Les Séquestrés d'Altona,* all in very fast French and interspersed with little grunts and incomprehensible jokes.

My French had improved considerably, but it was not up to the test of several strangers speaking at once about events of which I knew nothing. My head spun.

As the guests kept arriving, the big rooms grew warmer, the smells of cooking and flowers and perfume grew stronger, and the tight sash around my waist and the black ribbon around my neck seemed tighter.

Madame was no help. She, too, felt embarrassed. It was mortifying with all the guests here, that the host, whom they all expected, had not arrived, she murmured to me. What must they think? What could be keeping him?

Then abruptly, drawing on her ancient training, I suppose, she composed herself, took me by the hand, and led me over to the American couple from the château, the Hawthornes. I had seen the wife before, when she had come to buy a field. Now she was wearing a sensible beige silk, big flat white shoes, and short white gloves. Madame told them it was my birthday and said, "I will leave you all to speak English."

They peered at me through thick glasses, and I wondered what we could speak about. They asked politely how

I was enjoying my stay in the Loiret. "Once you've seen the castle at Yvres-le-Châtel, there is nothing much to see around here but wheat," the husband said. Madame had told me he had been a history professor at some famous university and was now writing a book about memory and France, something about how the French remembered the last war. "Heaven knows why he would want to write about that!" she had said dismissively.

He said, "Of course, at our age it's fine. I have my research, and Mary has her garden, but you must find it very quiet."

"Madame has taught me many things," I demurred. They looked quizzically at me. My words seemed to have troubled them.

"Have you met anyone your own age, dear?" the wife asked. I shook my head. The husband said something about the town of Pithiviers being somewhat off the beaten track. The wife, Mary — they were oddly, I remember, called William and Mary and laughed about the coincidence — complimented me on my dress. "Did you buy it in Paris?" she asked. I said Madame and I had found it in a store in Pithiviers. "Madame was kind enough to buy many nice things for me."

"I see," Mary said and looked at her husband. They both raised their eyebrows.

They asked me when I was planning on leaving, and if I were considering going on to college soon, perhaps even in the States? I said I didn't know, it was very far away, that I had done a *cours de civilisation Française* at the Sorbonne, and that I had been sent on down here for the summer.

William said, "But there are so many other places in
France you ought to see."

"Well, you have chosen Pithiviers yourselves, after all,"
I responded with a smile.

William looked at me and said, "Because of my work."
He appeared to hesitate and then added, "Surely you did
not know there was a concentration camp here during the
war?" I said I did know. I had heard something about it
from the cook, who was a terrible gossip.

Mary cleared her throat as Madame came over to us.
"She speaks lovely English," she told Madame. Madame
put her arm around my shoulder, gazed at me, and said,
"And she looks lovely, as she should on her eighteenth
birthday." I put my arm around Madame's waist and let my
head rest on her shoulder for a moment. I felt safe and
warm by her side, but I noticed how the Hawthornes
stared at us, concern in their shortsighted eyes.

I glanced through the open curtain just as Monsieur's
car came down the driveway. I saw Luis rush out and open
the door for him and confer with him for a moment in the
light from the windows. "I told you he'd come," I whispered to Madame, and she squeezed me closer to her side.

Then he was there, taller than the rest. We all looked up
as he approached, striding into his domain in a three-piece,
dove gray suit. I watched him approach, and waited to see
how he would greet me this time. He looked shiny to me:
his black shoes shone, his white forehead glinted, his fair
hair glistened with brilliantine. His gaze flickered, entering
into me for a moment and then passing on like a search-
light. He lifted his eyebrows slightly, his eyes taking in the

scene. His expression seemed to say, "I know you have all been expecting me; well, here I am; now you can relax and enjoy yourselves." He seemed to me a man of many secrets, his smooth pallor a mask to hide them all.

"What a pretty picture," he said amiably enough, looking at me and his wife together. He added, addressing his wife, "What a transformation in so short a time. Good work, Catherine."

I thought he, himself, looked transformed, younger, easier, and more self-assured. I knew that I would never forget the way he stood before us, smiling at me. He took my hand, squeezing my fingers until they hurt.

Madame drew him aside, speaking to him in a low voice, plucking at the collar of his suit nervously. Once again, I was struck by their similarity. It was not only that they looked suited to one another but rather that they were of one kind. Even the expression in the blue eyes was the same that night: she wanted him, I could see, to have a wonderful time; he, I realized, as I felt his gaze enter me again like water flowing through my veins, was dreaming of the same thing.

For the moment I was in love with both of them as I was with the heroes and heroines in the French books I had been reading: she was my Odette de Crecy, my Emma Bovary, my Madame de Rênal; he was my Swann, my Rodolphe, my Julien Sorel.

"Now you must take our little guest of honor in to dinner," Madame said. He took my arm and held me close to his side. I smelled his odor as he leaned down to whisper in my ear, "Are you having an amusing time, my dear?" I could only nod my head. "And how have you been since we last met?" he asked in a low voice. His banal questions seemed as intimate as a hand stroking, probing the depths, my heart of hearts. The words were almost obscene. "Fine, I've been fine," I said and stumbled on the steps. If he had not held me, I would have fallen. He clasped me tighter, and I felt myself lifted slightly, floating just above the floor. As we walked together, the guests gave way to us with merry greetings to Monsieur. We went up and up the steps into the dining room. The air was warm and fragrant with the scent of flowers and the odor of cooking beef and freshly ironed linen, and candle flames cast long gleams on the white brocade cloth, the silver, the cut glass, and the gold-rimmed plates. There were roses in rainbow colors in a long, low china bowl in the shape of a basket in the center of the table and starched napkins, erect like bishops' mitres, at each place with roses in the centers, yellow for the men and pink for the women.

"Sit here, my dear," Madame said and gave me the seat of honor in the middle of the table between Monsieur and the American professor, William. I felt the smile widen on my face.

Luis, in a white jacket and gloves, his hair plastered low across his forehead, waited at table with solemnity. His back had straightened, and he was filled with new dignity. He looked as though he were performing a ballet, dipping and rising on his toes around the table. He seemed pleased to be surrounded by all these notables in their finery. With one hand he delicately passed a tray of plump, pink-gray oysters in their pearly shells, while with the other he juggled a bottle of iced white wine, wrapped in a napkin. He followed this with Dolores's perfectly cooked beef Wellington on a silver dish, whisking off the shining cover with a quick, showy gesture and the gravity of a professor of black magic, bringing forth the pink and juicy beef in its pastry crust, surrounded by thin French beans, which brought exclamations of delight. Before the cake was brought in, he poured iced champagne into our glasses, holding one hand behind his back as though he were wounded.

I could not keep myself from stealing glances at Monsieur. I was studying his reaction, afraid that his amiability would alter, that he would glower, darken his eyes, grow somber at the thought of what this feast was costing him, at Madame's wild extravagance. But he appeared to be enjoying himself. He ate and drank heartily, joked with Luis, and flirted with the pretty, dark-haired woman on his left.

Nor did he ignore me. He would lean toward me and tell Luis to make sure my glass was filled or tell me to eat up or just pat my hand in a rather majestic and avuncular way. He would whisper to me. He complimented me on my dress, on the color of my cheeks, on my figure, as Madame had done, and as he spoke I felt an astonishing heat flicker up inside me. He said that the French countryside and his wife's company, winking across the table at her with complicity, had definitely been beneficial. "What a quick learner of French you are," he said. He wanted to know what I had heard from Mother. "Actually, I haven't heard from her at all. She hasn't sent me anything for my birthday. She is usually so generous," I confided.

And Monsieur leaned across the table and said something to Madame about a toast. Madame nodded her head but looked apprehensive, I thought, and rolled the dough from her bread roll between finger and thumb and bit on the side of her lip. Her cheek twitched. He tapped his cut-glass beaker and asked for quiet. He pulled down his gray silk waistcoat and stood with his back very straight. His pale face glowed beneficently as he first surveyed the long table and then looked down at me. The guests fell silent.

"My friends," he began. "Welcome to my home. What a joy it is to have you all here under my roof for such a happy occasion." As he spoke, Madame moved her lips, as though she were giving the speech for him. He went on, "I want to wish our little foreign guest, who has come from such a distance" — and he smiled down at me again, as though I were a long-lost child — "a happy birthday, for my part, for my wife's part, and from all of you assembled here." Everyone clapped, and I smiled up at him with tears in my eyes.

Once again I had the sensation of dreaming as I looked down the table at all these French people dressed in their finery for me, gathered here from some distance to celebrate the birthday of someone they did not know. Their strange, made-up faces grinned at me, as though we had known one another forever.

I thought the French were a splendid people: they had all the gifts; they were intelligent, clear-thinking, ironic; they had produced Descartes and the great classical dramatists Corneille and Racine; they were fun-loving and subtle humorists (I had attended Molière's plays at the Comédie-Française; I had applauded *Tartuffe*); they were gregarious, generous, and romantic (I could imagine Chateaubriand, his hair blowing in the wind, as he walked some windy hill in Brittany); their souls were deep (I had wept over Victor Hugo's poem about the death of his daughter). The great Flaubert, who had written the perfect novel, who knew all about life, was theirs.

Monsieur looked down at me tenderly. We waited for him to continue, listening to the hum of the river gliding under the old mill as it had been doing for hundreds of years.

"I have been asked to wish you a happy birthday from someone else, someone very dear to you," he went on. For one wild moment I thought of my sister and even imagined that she might make a last-minute entrance, pregnant as she was, perhaps leaning on her husband's arm; I caught myself looking toward the door, longingly.

"Your mother," Monsieur continued, "was the fairy godmother behind this feast. I want to drink a toast to her. I want to thank her for making this splendid party possible. My only regret this evening is that such a great and generous lady is not here to enjoy all of this." And he sat down beside me and knocked his glass against mine and drained it and gave me a kiss on my lips.

It was as if all the warm sweet sherry, all the iced white wine, all the cold champagne had rushed at once to my head, was beating in my ears. The table was swimming in wine, all its silver floating away on the tide, the gold-rimmed plates were gliding, the flowers, drifting. Madame's glossy pink lips were trembling, as if dissolved, watery, as I kissed Monsieur, went on kissing Monsieur, opening my lips greedily, deliberately prolonging the embrace, hearing the murmuring silence in the room.

When I looked at Madame, she was looking back at me, raising her thin eyebrows and her shoulders slightly as if to say, "How could I do otherwise, when your mother wanted it this way?"

"And the dresses, were they to be a surprise, too?" I asked, my head beginning to clear slightly.

It was Mother who had paid for this party. How could I have imagined that they would have done this for me?

I realized that the American professor, William, was talking to me, had been talking to me for a while. I turned toward him, so that Monsieur would not see the tears in my eyes.

He was telling me in a low voice in English that I might want to know what had happened in this place, that people here had been involved, and it might be best for me, under the circumstances, to spend my summer elsewhere.

Luis entered the room and dimmed the lights. Dolores followed him triumphantly in her white, frilled apron and cap, carrying the iced birthday cake aloft. "It looks like a wedding cake," the pretty woman said, as I felt Monsieur put his hand lightly but proprietorially on my knee.

All the guests sang loudly and somewhat drunkenly. As I blew out the candles in the half-light, I felt Monsieur's hand traveling up my leg, seeking me out, and all the while, the American was speaking and I was trying to hear what he was whispering so insistently to me.

Though the windows were open on the night, it seemed to me that there was no air in the room. Monsieur had inched his chair closer to mine, and the American was leaning toward me and murmuring on and on in my ear, "Of course, everyone must have known. It was in all the papers; it was right here, almost in the center of town, near the railway station," he said.

I felt Monsieur's hand slipping between my shaking thighs, and I thought, *His hand is touching me, his hand is touching me.* I caught a sort of mirthful expression on his face, but when next I glanced at him, he was not smiling and my heart was beating high and light in my throat like a trapped bird. And the American was going on talking.

"What, what?" I asked him impatiently.

"At the same time it was secret. Untalked about. Hushed up," he said.

I shifted my legs slightly and Monsieur slipped his fingers inside me.

"Abandoned children, little ones," the American whispered urgently in my ear.

"Why were they abandoned?" I said. "And what does this have to do with me?" I asked impatiently.

"Many of the people around here were implicated in different ways. They searched for jewelry, tore mothers from their children. They were told to go on ahead, to prepare. You could hear the screams for miles around," he said.

"Oh don't tell me, it's too horrible," I said, shaking my head. "I don't want to hear this," leaning toward Monsieur, feeling his fingers thrumming in my flesh and remembering words I had read:

Why did Maman have to throw herself at those two men's feet, begging them? It was so embarrassing, Maman on her knees, begging.

"Now, now, Madame, all will be well, if you remain calm and do as you are told to do," that soldier kept saying.

So embarrassing.

If only we had a photo of Maman.

"The Germans had never asked for anyone younger than sixteen," the professor continued. "Quite an irony, don't you think? German soldiers going through the cattle cars pulling off the younger children. Can you imagine?"

If only the German soldier had let us go with Maman on the train. Why did he say we were too young and had to get down from the train? We should have worn lipstick. If we'd worn lipstick maybe they would have thought we were old enough.

They would never have thought you were sixteen, silly. You don't even look twelve. And I would never have left you behind.

When the soldier grabbed us by the coat and pushed us out of the car, I kept seeing black spots spin before my eyes and my ears were ringing. Then the train was moving. I felt as if I were moving, swaying, drowning.

Where is Maman? I want to see Maman. I am frightened up here on our own. What will happen to us?

"What finally happened to them?" I asked.

"The French debated among themselves for a while, but finally demanded that the Germans take all the children, too. In the end they sent them off singing, two by two, telling them they were going to join their parents. Most of them, of course, did."

"And now we will dance," Monsieur said to me, taking my hand, leading me from the table, half-supporting me. We could hear the music swelling as he guided me down the steps and into the living room.

"I don't think I can. I feel sick," I murmured, the floor sinking and swelling, my whole body beating, and the words coming back to me:

I keep thinking of the little girl who could only say, I live at 12 bis.

Do you remember the little girl who had forgotten her name?

Most of the little ones had forgotten their names. Many of them couldn't even speak. Little ones who never smiled.

Monsieur was whispering in my ear, "You must not disappoint Madame. She only wanted to give you a splendid time. She has gone to so much trouble for you, for us," and I let him take me in his arms and turn me around.

But that little one who kept saying, over and over again, I live at 12 bis; I live at 12 bis. Don't you remember her? She must have been three years old.

He led me lightly into the familiar patterns I had learned at home. As I danced it all came back to me, the hot summer nights, the boys, their hair slicked back from their foreheads, their sweating hands, the warm, strong bodies pressed against mine, the whispered words, stumbling giggling through the grass, blackjacks catching in my stockings, going up the *koppie,* the deep velvet darkness and the burning of the stars above, crickets chirping, the howl of a dog, all the sounds of the night. I did not want to stop dancing. I wanted to be carefree. I wanted to forget the American's words, the words I had read. I wanted to live! Then, I became aware that everyone was standing around us, clapping as we danced. I let Monsieur turn me and twist me as Madame had done, my dress swirling around me.

7

I
T WAS DARK in my small room. Even if there had been
a lock on the door, I do not believe I would have used
it at that moment. I was waiting, listening to the hard,
dry wind in the leaves of the willows and the ominous roll
of distant thunder and the music that still played in my
head. My host came to my door, as I knew he would, as I
had wanted him to. Even so, I was as terrified as I had been
when he had appeared before in the attic. I was unable to
move, to cry out.

Looking back, I see myself lying on the narrow bed
with its long, French bolster. I turn on the bedside lamp,
making shadows fall from the heavy armoire, the table
with the magazines. I am in my pink cotton nightgown
with the buttons down the front, all the makeup removed
from my eyes, thin lips, and childish cheeks. My arms are
smooth, tanned from all the sun and the walks across those
flat French fields. My hair is loose and shiny from washing.
Beads of perspiration mark my upper lip. My head pounds,
my mouth is dry from excitement and champagne, my

body trembles, as though I were still dancing, as though Monsieur's fingers were still inside me.

There he is. The light flickers in his large eyes, on his glistening lips, in his fair hair like a light cloud above his head, and in his navy silk dressing gown belted at the waist, and on what I catch among the folds: his nakedness. The door is open behind him, and for a moment I think I see a shadow on the stairs. Is it Luis?

"Leave me alone," I mutter.

"Nonsense," he says, as though reprimanding a recalcitrant child, "no hysterics, please." He sits down in the chair facing me, impassive, calm. The shadows lick at his face. For a moment he looks tired, old, I think. His nose seems sharp, longer. As always I see the similarity with his wife. As in a drunkard's vision, they are two and yet one: the smooth, pale, skin, the quick glimpse of the uneven, bluish teeth, the distant air.

He leans toward me, pats my hand reassuringly. "I just came to see if you were all right, dear. Are you thirsty? Would you like a bottle of water? We are quite selfish, Madame and I — we admit it, and we could see you were sad. We don't like children to be sad." He goes on stroking my hand in a soothing, fatherly way that it would be ungrateful to reject. I hear a movement on the stairs. Is it Madame? Who is out there listening in the dark?

I look at him and think he is not what I thought: he looks rather foolish, with a scarf around his long neck, his lips crimson. Who is this stranger? What moves him?

"What about Madame?" I ask, glowering at him.

"Catherine, too, only wants your happiness. She has tried so hard to please you, after all."

"Has she? She wasn't the one who provided the party," I say, sulkily.

"What difference does it make who provided the means? We provided what we could. Catherine was the one who did the work, after all. She spent the time and the trouble, and surely that is what counts. She even spent some of her own money, my dear. I was quite cross. She did all those lovely flowers for you. She invited all our friends for you, people from illustrious families — the de La Tour d'Auvergnes, the de Montesquieus! Some would give the eyes of their heads to meet people of that sort. She is a generous woman, my wife, in every way."

"Why don't you go to *her* bed then?" I say, but I know that sounds childish, jealous, ungrateful, somehow wrong, and I have the bizarre and frightening feeling not so much that I do not know who he is, but that I am not sure who I am, or rather who this girl is sitting in this strange bed with this strange man beside her.

He laughs at me and squeezes my hand. "In France, you see, among the upper classes it is rather different," he explains. "We don't rush off to get divorced every five minutes, the way you Anglo-Saxons do. We leave each other a little liberty, as married people must, if they have any sense. We sleep in separate rooms, sometimes even in separate houses for a while. Why not? Married people have desires like everyone else's, after all. We see a pretty girl or boy. We each go our own way, but we respect one another deeply, and we are great friends. We tell one another everything, well, almost everything. And don't think we are not lovers, too, oh yes, we are, passionately so — not like those awful, dull Anglo-Saxon marriages, where no one says a word at breakfast, and everyone is bored to tears. It all goes much better this way, for everyone," he says, smiling and slipping his hand through the short sleeve of my gown, up my arm, and cupping my shoulder.

"I know Madame is unhappy, that she misses you," I insist.

"Of course, and that is why she is so happy to see me. Passion can only exist with absence. Absence makes the heart grow fonder, as you say," he adds in his execrable English. "What do you want, *poupée?* If I were here all the time, she would be bored; that's the truth," he adds with a shrug.

"You don't always tell the truth, though. What about the camp here?" I say, thinking of William's words, the words in *La Semaine de Suzette.*

>*I keep seeing that hand.*
>   *What hand?*
>   *That little girl who had stuck her fingers through the slats in the train and the way the gendarme hit them.*

He draws himself up, looking into the distance. "Ah, I see our Professor William has been talking to you. Americans are very naïve, puritanical, are they not? They know little about life, about our life. They can afford to be moralistic. They did not fight the war on their own soil. I can imagine him talking to you about what we did in the war. We should not judge others in situations we have never been in, that we cannot even imagine. How can you be so sure how *you* would have behaved? And what about your own country, my dear? Your countrymen have hardly covered themselves with glory."

I lower my gaze and recall the African servant at home who spends his time polishing the floors, and the lines of black people waiting for buses in the streets of Johannesburg at the end of the day.

"How do you know what this place was like at that time? Would you have acted heroically? Because only heroes could have done anything. We tried that in the First World War, but we lost. I received the Croix de Guerre for bravery when I was not much older than you are now, *bébé*. Experience has made us a practical people. Sometimes that is the kinder way. What could we have done for those little children without their parents? Everyone thought they would be reunited. No one could imagine what would happen."

I think then of the words I had read and reread, trying to make sense of them.

How much longer will we have to stay up here?

As long as you can look out the window and see the trees, the bird's nest, a sparrow perched on a branch, the river running under the house. Everything is alive, don't you see — each trembling leaf, each drop of water, even the tiniest insect. Everything will go on living: the leaves will be beautiful here next summer.

"You know what my wife said to me, just tonight?" he asks me, and gives my shoulder a squeeze. "The problem with our lovely little paying guest is she takes everything too seriously."

He goes on, "She thinks you're just a bit of a prude, you see," he says and reaches over to rub the tense muscles of my shoulders comfortingly with one hand and with the other strokes my neck.

"Is that so?" I say, feeling a warm languor spreading from my neck to my breasts, my nipples hardening. I want to explain myself to him. "I've been so unhappy. I want so to be happy," and a tear runs down the hollow between my cheekbone and my nose.

"Of course you do, of course you do. And so you should, and will — that I can promise you. We will take my old Porsche and go on the road together, just you and me. We will see the Sound and Light at Chenonceaux. We will picnic on the grass at Azay, and I will tell you all about the places: the people, the kings, their mistresses, their lovers," he says. He pats my back and wipes my cheeks with the clean handkerchief he takes from his pocket. He whispers in my ear, "You have had a bad time, cocotte. Someone has been careless, some boy, perhaps? Now that is not a crime — all young people are careless. We are too old for that."

"My sister told you what happened?" I ask, weeping even louder at this further betrayal.

He pushes me over with a little familiar shove of his hip and sits beside me on the narrow bed, propping his back up against the wall, kicking off his slippers, crossing his legs, his feet white and narrow. He puts an arm around my shoulders amicably, as my sister used to do in the dormitory at boarding school. He strokes my hair gently. I lean against him, let the tears fall.

"You would like to feel sorry for yourself, I understand. We all do. We want to feel aggrieved, but we mustn't, my dear. It's a waste of time, just as it is to blame someone for what happened here during the last war. No one was at fault, certainly not us — on the contrary."

I had such a beautiful dream last night. I saw it quite clearly: the Rue des Rosiers, the windows of the apartment with the gray shutters thrown back. Maman was at the window with her hair parted on the side and left loose on her shoulder, and Papa was standing behind her. He had his pipe in one hand, and they were both waving to me. Maman said quite distinctly, "Come back, come back in, Anna, it's all been a mistake."

"And what happened tonight was not my wife's fault. Your mother wrote and told her to keep the money a secret and to use it for a party. It seemed a lot of money, but that was what your mother wanted. She is extravagant, generous, kind. We had to ask *our* friends. Whom else, after all? Your friends are far away," he says, holding me closer.

"I have had such a bad time. My sister's husband was so cross with me: he's such a horrible snob." I weep loudly.

"A French bourgeois snob? A doctor, not so? There is nothing worse than that, I assure you, and I can just hear him saying Monsieur le Baron, this, and Monsieur le Baron, that."

I cannot help laughing at this accurate description of Jean Luc. "I bet he likes the sound of a title," Monsieur says, laughing and leaning forward right and left as though bowing, making me laugh and cry at the same time.

"Oh, he *is* horrible. He took me to a horrible doctor. I almost died. The *sage-femme* refused to give me any anesthesia, because she said that way I wouldn't be so careless again. She hurt me so, and they said I was disgraceful, had disgraced them."

"Now, now. Of course you had not. You are young and adventurous. Your boyfriend was careless, that's all, and your family has been unkind. They are prudes and hypocrites. We know the type. Forget them. Some people are not gifted at happiness. They should have taken your part, but at least, thanks to them, you are here with us. It is all turning out well. We are not prudes and hypocrites. We understand people, and we will be honest with you, basically honest, which does not mean to say that everything we tell you is true," he says, pressing against me and rubbing his hand slowly and softly in my hair, gently circling my neck, his eyes glittering, his breathing labored.

I wipe the tears from my cheek and lean against him, my body weary and warm. My heart is going madly, and his mouth is near mine.

"But you must help me, too, darling. I know you will be generous and good to me. I have fallen so for you, for all your bright, young loveliness. It is impossible to resist. It is stronger than I am. It drives me to despair. I cannot sleep or rest without you. I am so tired. I need to see you. Just one little look," he says, turning toward me, pursing his lips like a child, and unbuttoning my nightgown to expose my breasts.

"You are so kind and generous and passionate," he

whispers, his lips close against my ear, his hands cupping my breasts, rolling my nipples. "Why struggle against passion? Is it not the source of everything beautiful? Of art and song? We are above petty, bourgeois thinking. Look at your breasts — how beautiful they are."

I look down and see my breasts as if for the first time, and the sight of them excites me.

"Madame wants you to help me. It means nothing to her. It will help her, too."

Each time he touches me I feel as if I am rising into the air with a little surge.

"You don't really want me to go away, do you?" he asks, lifting my chin to make me look at him. Do I want him to go away? No, I don't. I don't. I look back at his smooth skin, light blue eyes, high white forehead, full lips. His skin smells of the mysterious odor of childhood.

He lowers his head to my breasts and his mouth finds my nipple and he stays there flooding me and I hear the river running beneath us and the wind beating the shutter back and forth and outside I can see the branches pushing against the glass.

The apple tree and the cherry will be white with blossoms. The petals will stir and perfume the air. The sky will be infinitely blue. How wonderful it would be to lie in the grass and look up at it.

What will happen to us if they find us up here?

"Just do this one little thing for me," he coaxes, opening his gown more and moving himself against my leg. "Help me, please, to ease my suffering. No one else can help me now," he murmurs urgently and guides my hand to where he wants it, rubbing it up and down, making gasping sounds. "Yes, yes, you are good and generous. Yes, yes, that is my good, good girl," he keeps saying, and I close my eyes and see not his blue, hooded ones but Richard's quick brown ones, and I hear the rustling of Richard's blue raincoat, but it is Monsieur who gives a long, satisfied sigh.

He takes out the handkerchief that has dried my eyes and wipes himself and draws himself up, adjusting his robe. He rises and walks to the door, leaving me alone with my body crashing wildly like water falling into the dark.

8

I FELT A HAND on my shoulder. When I turned over and looked up. I saw her standing there in a diamond of early morning light.

My lips were dry, and my head ached. I had dreamt of lying in Richard's arms until his brown eyes, wide grin, and slight sex became the blue eyes, the lips, and full sex of Monsieur, who was once again wiping the flow with his white handkerchief.

The thin curtain flapped like a white veil. Madame was carefully made up, her cheeks heavily rouged, her mouth a savage pink, her blue eyes glittering, her face hard and cold and suddenly aged, as though the air had escaped from under her skin. She was exquisite and regal, but she was older, I realized, than I had thought. It was a face that was not kind: it was clear and sharp and quick. There was something brittle about her I had not noticed before. She wore a tight yellow-green taffeta suit, which showed off her shapely legs. I felt a constriction of the heart, as I smelled her cloying lily scent.

She was saying, "I need a second opinion. What do you think of the outfit?" turning around.

"Oh, very nice, Madame," I replied, pulling myself up in my bed.

She let out a harsh, mirthless laugh. She told me she was having Luis drive her up to Paris for a few days, and she hoped I could cope on my own. Could I keep an eye on the house for her? Could I walk the dog? Dolores was exhausted after last night and was never much help with the dog. She didn't like animals or children. Madame was convinced that in her absence Dolores kept the dog chained in the doghouse outside.

I did not have time to reply.

She added, "Oh, I almost forgot," and took a package wrapped in tissue paper from the quilted handbag that hung on a gold chain from her shoulder. "I brought you something to wear with your white dress, a present, from me this time," and she placed the package beside me. Impatiently, she opened it for me, taking out a white silk scarf.

"Oh, thank you," I said dully, without looking at her, but taking the scarf. She went toward the door, tapping in her high-heeled shoes, her stockings brushing against her thighs. "Madame," I called out.

"What is it?" she asked, her hand on the doorknob.

"I want to talk to you," I said.

"Can't it wait until I get back? I'll only be gone a few days, dear. Luis has the car ready for me. I have an important appointment," she said coldly over her shoulder.

"It won't take long," I said and drew myself up further on the bed, clasping my knees to my chest. "I want to leave, and the sooner the better. I have to ask you for some of the money Mother sent."

"There is none left. Your mother sent a very generous check, but she wanted it spent on the party. Splendid, wasn't it?"

I nodded grimly.

"Besides, I couldn't give you money even if there were some. It wouldn't be right, would it? Your mother doesn't want you to leave."

"That's not fair. You should have asked me what I wanted to do with it," I said, but all the time I was thinking it was perfectly useless, I knew this woman would never let me go.

She looked offended and said, "Yes, I enjoyed spoiling you, as I would have a daughter of my own. We got a bit carried away with the dresses, didn't we? But you can't go off on your own, darling. Your mother would be worried about you. Your sister doesn't want you in Paris, I gather. Guy doesn't want you to leave, and I can't just let you go, do you see. Besides, where would you go? If I have understood rightly, you have already got into enough mischief." Her mouth was suspicious, hard and shrewd.

"Anywhere! I would go anywhere!" I shouted at her.

"That's the point. You'd be reckless and silly; you'd be hysterical and childish. And all of this because Guy has been making love to you. Oh, yes, I know. I know what you two were doing last night. I was outside the door, listening."

"How could you do that?" I exclaimed.

"You would have done the same, don't you think, if it was your husband, a husband you loved deeply?" she replied, her voice trembling slightly, her little hands moving up to touch her hair. "You cannot know how much I love him," she added, and her voice broke, and her blue eyes filled with tears.

"I want to go! I want to go!" I shouted at her helplessly. I was confounded by these people. Nothing made any sense to me anymore. The bright morning light on Madame's face showed me what I had never seen before, how false she was, and how she had lipstick smudged on her thin, blue-white teeth.

I thought of the words in *La Semaine de Suzette.*

Do you remember the women at the window who clapped when they took us away?
   Even Madame Rochat was there clapping to see them rounding up the Jews.

You have stolen my money. You have betrayed me twice. I wanted to shout at her, but she came over to the bed, gave me her handkerchief, and sat down in the chair, as her husband had done the night before. She crossed her slim legs, drawing her skirt up to reveal her pink knees, gleaming beneath an edge of laced, silk petticoat. She patted my hand in the reassuring way he had and kissed me on my cheek.

She said it was obvious that her husband was infatuated with me. There was nothing she could do about that. And I had not really improved matters, had I? She did not blame me for flirting with him, dancing with him, but was it necessary to do it so blatantly, in front of all her guests? Everyone could see that I was falling for him. Could I deny it?

"Then lend me a little money and let me go," I begged abjectly.

"He would only come after you, if you tried to leave," she said, pulling a kid glove onto her hand, smoothing the creases, pushing down the material between her fingers. "He wants to make love to you. That's the way it is. Of course, it will only last for a moment, you understand. It never lasts long with him. But when he wants something, it is better that he gets it," she said and made a gesture of finality, her pale gloved hand moving flat and firm through the air.

"But what about me?" I asked.

"Of course I was a fool to confide in you, to be so good to you, but there's no point in your going off now."

"I want to go away! I don't want to see your husband again; I don't want to see you again!" I shouted at her and beat my fists against my knees like a small child.

"Why don't you talk this over with Guy while I am away, dear. I really have to go now. Let's remain friends, you and I."

"I want to go," I said in a low, mournful voice.

"And what would you do if you left, my child? You'd end up doing something silly, like dancing topless in some cabaret, or being knifed by some Arab in a dark back street," she said and shuddered slightly.

For some reason her words made me laugh: the vision of me dancing topless in a cabaret.

She added in her most matter-of-fact French voice, "Don't take everything so seriously. Haven't you any sense of humor? Anyway, you can't go until I get back from Paris, there's no one to walk the dog. Wait until I get back. I've got something important I have to do in Paris, someone I have to consult, and then we'll see what can be done. It's the least you can do for me, after all I have done for you."

I could hear the sound of her high heels clicking on the stairs, the front door slamming, and the car moving across the pebbles of the courtyard.

I rose and watched the black car gain speed and disappear. I picked up the cameo, which was still lying on the table by my bed. The face did not look like Madame's: the hair curly, the eyes full of mystery. Surely Madame owed me something as well? I slipped it into the pocket of my dressing gown and lay back and turned my face to the green linen wall. I felt the dog jump up onto the bed with one quick bound and settle his warm, heavy body against me.

9

I WENT BACK TO SLEEP and slept late. When I woke the room was full of light and seemed larger. The garden lay dreaming in its impossible loveliness, hardly a garden, more the idea of a garden, with its banks of bright daisies, transparent roses, silver willows, and the sinuous ribbon of a river.

Dolores's failure to bring me breakfast was a bad sign. Perhaps she had been told to stay away, or she may merely have remained in her cottage, sleeping, after her exertions of the previous day. Whatever the reason, the silence in the house bereft of her bustling, garrulous presence seemed ominous.

It was another white-hot July day. Nothing moved in the still air. Even the dog remained lying listlessly on my bed, panting. There was no sign of anyone, though I could see Monsieur's dark green Porsche like a shadow.

Breathlessly, I pushed my clothes into my backpack, leaving most of the new garments Madame had bought hanging in the closet. I put on a tight pink skirt and white blouse and made up my face in an abbreviated duplication of Madame's artistry.

I descended into the quiet hall and walked through the big, silent, sun-flecked rooms. I had the sensation of floating underwater through the silence like a sea creature wafted by the current. Water sounded in my ears.

I saw no sign of Monsieur. I assumed he was still sleeping. I picked up the telephone in the hall without compunction and called Cecile. An unfamiliar voice informed me that my sister was in the American Hospital and that she had had a baby girl the night before. They had called the baby Deidre, after me, because she was born on my birthday.

"Ah, you are Dodo," Jean Luc's mother said, identifying herself. She explained, faintly disapprovingly, that she had come to render the service I might have fulfilled, the care of little Pierre. I heard his cry in the background, and asked if I could speak to him, but the woman refused.

I remembered that it would be impossible to call Mother from the house. I would have to trudge into the post office in Pithiviers to make a call of that kind. There was only one person I could call: Richard. I hadn't spoken to him for months, and I hesitated, but what else could I do? His voice was faint. "Did you get all my letters?" I asked.

"What letters?" he shouted.

I told him that I missed him and had written several times to tell him about this place, these strange people, that I thought of him often. Why did he not come down to see me? Why had he not even called?

"You never gave me your number, and when I called

your sister to get it, she refused to give it to me. So I haven't heard from you for months. Now you expect me to rush down immediately. Where are you, anyway?"

I told him, and he said he had worked once in a hotel on the main square. I tried to imagine him approaching us in his shiny blue raincoat and its matching beret, coming across the smooth lawn as Madame looked him up and down.

"I can't come down there now," he replied. "I'm busy for the next couple of weeks. I'm involved in an important project, something that might turn out to be very lucrative."

"I need to see you. I need to talk you about something urgently," I said a little desperately.

There was a silence on the other end.

"Who are these people you're staying with, anyway?" he finally broke in, and when I gave him their names, he said, "Oh, I have heard of them somewhere or the other."

"We could meet in the village nearby, in Estouy, if you don't want to come here," I said.

He gave in as I had hoped he would.

I shut the dog in the garden and left the house as I had arrived, in the early afternoon, my backpack over my shoulder. I walked fast in the heat, looking for any sign of Monsieur. I was panting a little as I climbed the steep hill past the shack where the poor children lived. This time it was shut up and quiet.

I have always wondered how French villages can look so deserted, all the shutters closed and no one in the streets. Where do all the people go? That afternoon Estouy looked like a stage set for such a village.

I walked on in the glare, passing the old, yellow gas

pump with its blank shell face. My tight skirt hindered my legs. I was acutely conscious of my physical presence, but not quite sure who I was, if anyone. By leaving the mill I seemed to have stepped out of my existence. Part of me wanted to return to Monsieur, but, as in a dream, I was dragged forward by the need to know what would happen next, as I had been on my arrival in that place.

Then I heard a clicking behind me, drawing closer, the sound of nails on the road. I spun around to see the dog, his smooth, dark coat shining in the sun. How had he escaped? He must have burrowed a hole under the fence, because he was coming up to me panting, tongue lolling, ears flapping. I shouted at him to go home, waved my hand, even tried to push him in that direction, but he resisted my efforts, snarling at me. I left him sitting up expectantly, ears pricked, at the door of the general store on the small square in Estouy and went in to wait for Richard.

I thrust my hand into the pocket of my skirt and counted out the little change I had left. It seemed cool and dark inside. There was an assortment of objects and smells: the long thin caramels in yellow wrappers, the odors of soap and tobacco, and the old, yellowed postcards, curling up at the edges in a revolving rack, which creaked as I turned it.

I drifted into the smoky back room, where the drinks were sold, watching the workmen in their blue, paint-spattered overalls, playing pool and drinking the local red wine in small, thick wineglasses. They stared at me, and I lowered my gaze, conspicuous and embarrassed. A stout man offered me a Gauloise. I was certain he must have taken me for a prostitute. I had never smoked, never even liked the smell of the smoke, but I took it and let him light it for me, coughing as I stared at the mark of pink lipstick.

I kept my eyes on the door. Would Richard ever come? And if he did come, what would I say to him exactly? Did I want to go back to Paris with him? Did I really intend to leave the mill?

The bells rang as someone opened the door. At first I hardly recognized him. He had grown a reddish beard, and his face looked longer, his eyes deeper-set and closer than I remembered. His lips looked pink and vulnerable, and when he kissed me on the cheek, in the French way, I did not recognize his smell, and I drew back from him. He was not wearing his rustling raincoat, and his shoes, I noticed, looked worn and dusty, the toes slightly upturned.

Richard bought a bottle of the slightly sweet red wine that is made nearby, and we sat down at a table by the window. He filled our glasses, lifted his to the light, so that it seemed to glow. He swilled the liquid around a little, spilling some onto the table. He said I looked as if the country air had been good for me.

I said I wanted to leave the place, but as I did so, I thought, No, I don't want to, I cannot go.

Richard said, "Good. I was afraid that couple would not let you come."

I wanted to know what he had heard about them, but Richard wanted to talk about me. I asked him about himself. Nothing had changed, I gathered, after all. He was still working in the dark well behind the desk in the foyer of a small hotel in the Latin Quarter, with the keys hanging on the wall and the smell of clogged drains.

Finally he got around to the point that preoccupied me. "The husband must be a terrible snob, and the wife even worse," Richard said.

I interrupted him, "I think she hates me. What is so awful is that she pretends to like me, do you see?" I said.

"Typical," I remember Richard saying, adding something like "Those people were probably collaborators."

"Nonsense. How could they be? Monsieur was in the Résistance," I remonstrated. It was all right for me to criticize, but I did not like him doing so. I suspected he was jealous.

"Lots of people claimed to be, particularly toward the end of the war, when they could see which way the wind was blowing. But I read somewhere that they were suspected of receiving Germans during the war — lots of aristocrats did. They invited them into their homes, threw big parties for them."

"That's not possible," I retorted, but I could easily imagine the scene: the Germans arriving, tall and slim, their eyes the color of their impeccable uniforms, the cinched waists, the sharp epaulets, all spilling out of the cars, stamping out their cigarettes with the heels of narrow, shining boots before lifting the knocker. I saw Dolores open the door in her white apron and cap, squinting ingratiatingly. I imagined Monsieur in his black tie and shiny black shoes and Madame in her sequined black evening dress, her fine, fair hair falling over her shoulders, standing in the hall, smiling, welcoming them graciously.

"The German aristocracy is the oldest of all, did I know?" It was her highest compliment.

Richard asked me if I knew about the camp here. I nodded. What had he heard about it? I asked.

He had a friend who lived in Pithiviers, who remembered seeing those children, hundreds of them, roaming back and forth like little ghosts. His friend had walked past the camp with his school, but the teacher had said nothing about the children, just turned his eyes away.

I told Richard about the writing I had found in the attic in the margins of the old book, a sort of conversation, as if two people were talking in writing.

"Did you ever hear of any children who had survived the camp?" I asked him.

He shook his head and said he did not know much about it, and changed the subject. He wanted me to leave Pithiviers and join him in Paris, but as he talked to me of his life, I thought of the words written so long ago.

I keep hearing the sound of the mothers' cries, like the cries of animals. I see them rolling on the ground, adults, rolling on the ground and beating their heads against the ground! And the children making peepee in their pants.

At least they did not strip Maman and push her under the shower.

Or kick her and make her open her legs to look for jewels.

That crazy woman was screaming, "They are going to kill us all!"

She wasn't a crazy woman.

I think Maman will be waiting for us, wondering where we are. If only we knew where she was. I was so frightened when the German soldier made us get off the train. I am so frightened up here when it's dark.

"Do you think any of those children might have escaped?" I interrupted to ask again, imagining the names entwined with flowers and clinging vines: Anna and Lea, Leanna, Annalea, Liane. Were they two or one? How had they come to be in the de C's attic?

He shrugged and said that none of those who knew the whole story would tell it, that it was hushed up, naturally, and that it had happened a long time ago. He reiterated his suggestion to leave the place, to come back to Paris with him.

I keep telling you we are better off where we are. Didn't you see what it was like in the train! How could they pack so many people into such a small space? We are safe and dry up here, and we have enough to eat. Don't worry, Lea, I'm going to take care of you. I'm going to make sure they don't put us back on that train. We will be safe here if you are quiet and good, if you don't drive me mad. It is dry and warm, and there are no rats.

I looked at his young face, the freckled nose. I thought of Monsieur saying, "Your boyfriend was careless." Could I go back to Richard's little room and roll around on his narrow bed? Could I live with him? Could I find some sort of work in this foreign country whose language I had not yet mastered? Should I call Mother and ask her to send me a ticket home? But did I want to go back to South Africa?

He took my hand, looked into my eyes, and said that I had never looked as good, that I should always make my eyes up that way. He said he had missed me, worried about me, felt awful about what had happened. He was so sorry he had not been able to help me.

We moved to the back of the room and sat down in the dim light on the old sofa. My skirt slipped up my damp thighs. He kissed me on the lips this time, tasting of wine and tobacco. I had never been kissed by a man with a beard. It pricked, not unpleasantly, and I put my hand to my cheek. There were rooms upstairs. He'd be happy to take one; we could spend the night there and take the bus up to Paris in the morning. He would do whatever I wanted to do. He kissed me again and shut his eyes and ran his wide hands over my face, my breasts, my thighs, as though he no longer remembered how they felt or as though he were blind. I could feel his warm, soft body, the swelling of his sex.

Suddenly the dog began barking furiously outside. I looked out the window to see Monsieur standing there. Absurdly, like a child, I felt my heart hammer with a mixture of fear and excitement and my palms begin to sweat.

He came striding into the room with the dog behind him. There was a moment of silence when the workmen stopped playing pool and lifted their heads to watch him and stare at the dog as it ran over to me, barking at Richard. Then the hum of conversation and the clicking of the balls resumed.

He stood before the counter, tall and elegant, jangling his change in the pocket of his perfectly cut tweed jacket,

and asking for a packet of cigarettes from the woman behind the counter. He made no sign of having seen me, but
when he had made his purchase, he turned his head and
whistled for the dog, holding open the glass door and setting off the bells above the door. Then he raised his finely
arched eyebrows at me expectantly.

Everyone in the room was watching us. I moved slightly
away from Richard, who still had his arm around my
shoulder, and the dog slumped down heavily against my
legs. I leaned forward and patted his head. Monsieur shut
the door behind him, walked over to me, bent toward me,
and said in a low but insistent tone, "Don't make a scene.
Just come outside. I need to talk to you."

We stood opposite the town hall, its cluster of faded tri-
color flags flying in the wind that had risen. We argued in
the small square by the old church while the dark leaves of
the chestnut trees shook. A ruby sun was setting, and the
garish orange glow lit up the sky like a conflagration. The
wind blew, and we shouted, and the dog, as though wish-
ing to join in, barked at my feet.

"Shut up," I said to the dog.

"This is really not the sort of place for a young girl,"
Monsieur scolded, his face red.

"I couldn't care less," I shouted, or something rather
ruder than that in French.

"What on earth would your mother say? What were
you doing? I didn't know where you were. I was worried
out of my mind."

"It's none of your business," I said, but I noticed for the

first time a faint bluish gleam of beard just beneath the pink skin. He must have left the house in a hurry.

"Workers, only working men go in there. It's not a place for a decent young girl. You don't understand, because you're not French," Monsieur explained, shaking his head.

"My friend, Richard, came down from Paris to talk to me. We are going away," I said, lifting my chin at him.

Monsieur put his hands to his head and said, "From me? From us? Why? You know I'm crazy about you. You can't go away with that little common man — what is he, some sort of concierge? I don't want you seeing him again, do you understand! Never. I have never shared a woman with another man, and I'm not going to start now with one of that sort. I'll do whatever you want. If you must go, I'll drive you to Pithiviers, myself, I'll drive you up to Paris to your sister," he exclaimed wildly, his eyes glittering.

In the distance we could hear the low roll of thunder, and clouds passed quickly across the sky. I stood there sulking, my head down, trying to hold on to my anger, not knowing quite why I was angry anymore. I knew there was something wrong with what he was saying, but I was losing interest in finding out what it was.

"Well, come on then, come on," he urged, adopting his fatherly tone anew and picking up my backpack. He slung it over his shoulder, adding, "My God, this is heavy. What have you got in here? Gold bars?"

I heard the door of the general store slam shut and watched Richard come out and stand for a minute in the doorway. He looked at me inquiringly, and I looked back, biting my lip, not knowing what to do. He looked so young standing next to Monsieur. I noticed his nose was a little red. I shook my head and shrugged my shoulders at him helplessly. He stalked away from us. He did not even look back over his shoulder at me.

"There's no bus until the morning, anyway. What were you going to do here all night?" Monsieur added, jerking his head back to indicate Richard. "Let me take you out somewhere good for dinner, and then we will do whatever you want."

He took my hand and said, "We both needed to get out of that house. We needed a change, to talk."

I withdrew my hand but followed him along the street. The sun was setting as we walked down the hill past the shack where the poor children lived. The sturdy boy in his short gray pants and the girl in a ragged pink dress were running down the road away from their mother, who stood in the road with the switch in her hands, grinning at us, showing her missing teeth.

"You should leave them alone," I shouted over my shoulder at her as we went by.

Then we were walking in silence, holding hands. Mauve flowers pushed their way through the ancient stones of the walls, and the sky was pink and gray, and chickens clucked as they waddled down the road. It was almost dark by the time we reached the mill, and the trees were rustling in the wind, and the house seemed to float toward us with all the lights lit like a great stone boat, empty and silent and haunted.

"I know a good place in Pithiviers," he said, adding, "Wear your white dress, will you?"

Part Two

→>←←

10

READING BACK over what I have written, in this quiet room high above the city, it seems to me that I have drawn a portrait of the Baron de C that is misleading. It is difficult, after so many years, to convey the essence of his charm: for he was the most charming man I ever met. Though I was destined never to see him again after that summer, he made my life impossible from then on, because I could not help comparing every man I encountered to him. He was a clever conversationalist. His French was different from Madame's, a little slower, perhaps for my benefit, with less of an English pronunciation, fewer English words, but clearer, each sentence brilliantly clear and to the point. Perhaps what I loved more than anything was just to hear him speak French. It was not that he was learned, though he may have been more so than he pretended to be. He once told me that he had been given a Distinction on his baccalaureate in French, without having read any of the books; he had simply read summaries. Nevertheless, he would make certain generalizations that led me to believe he had read insightfully, that he had an original mind. He would say, "The main theme in French literature is not love but money. After all, why does Madame Bovary die? And what about Balzac? Even Voltaire writes mainly about money. Did you know he won the lottery, invested the proceeds, and became a millionaire?"

However, much of his charm lay in his capacity to remain silent and to listen. There was nothing passive about that. He listened so closely that he seemed to understand my halting sentences before I had completed them, almost before they had begun. He transformed my banal, childish words into something witty and amusing; moreover, he was always capable of finding something positive, beneficial, and redeeming in my experiences. Though I was later to learn how deep his pessimism ran, on the surface he was most reassuringly optimistic.

When I said my sister left me to my own devices to wander around the Parisian streets in the rain, he said that it was probably better that I took my first steps toward independence, after the sheltered existence I had led. When I complained that my mother had not written to me but had only sent a check for my birthday, he called her a wise woman, who apparently knew that actions speak louder than words. He was full of maxims of that sort, which, when I look back, seem ironic. He said that talk was cheap, but, to me, his was worth a fortune.

Like all the highborn French, he knew just which wine to order, which dish to choose, at which hotel to stop, and though I was never quite sure who was paying for these items (did Mother's check cover dinner, and all that followed?) I enjoyed them with him.

We parked his ancient Porsche beneath a chestnut tree on the main square in Pithiviers, entered under the arched doorway, and crossed the courtyard of the hotel, which must once have been a hunting lodge. I remember its big, half-empty dining rooms: the blood red tablecloths, the black beams, the stiff arum lilies, the carnations in silver flutes, a thin waitress with a long, severe face, and the stuffed heads of deer on the walls, their empty, glassy eyes staring down at us mournfully.

While we drank an apéritif he talked about himself. He amused me with tales of war and love, all told in a self-deprecating manner, as though he had blundered in a shell-shocked daze into acts of extraordinary bravery and stumbled unwittingly from these into endless sex. He told me about the battle of the Marne, for which he had been decorated. He spoke fondly of his exploits with women. "Ah," he said, speaking of one of them, opening his arms wide, "with her, anything went."

He told me of his role in the Résistance: how he had swum across freezing rivers, his clothes in a bundle over his head; how once he had burned documents in a bathroom, the smoke emanating from the window and arousing someone to fetch the fire brigade; how he had gone to England to join de Gaulle and had parachuted back into France, dropping through the dark into a tree and breaking his leg, afterward dragging himself across a field, only to be picked up by peasants who turned him over to the authorities. He told me how he had convinced Klaus Barbie to allow a woman into the Gestapo prison, ostensibly to marry one of the Jewish prisoners on grounds of morality — the woman was pregnant — which enabled him then to help the prisoner escape. He told me the name they had given him: Dash.

I wondered if I had not read a similar account in a book. Was he making it all up?

He ordered a delicious *turbot hollandaise avec pommes vapeur.* The white wine was cold and bubbly, and as I began to eat, I became aware of how hungry I was. Without my even having to ask him about the children in the attic, he told me about them.

He explained that there had been two children who had come to the mill to ask for help one night during the war. He and Madame were already living there in the summer of '42. "In those days one used a pontoon to get to the house and garden. The bridge had not been built. The river was deeper and ran faster. It has shrunk since then, for some reason — perhaps the pollution."

He was not sure how the girls had access to the garden. They seemed so slight and so weary, he was not certain that they could have maneuvered the pontoon. They had made their way undetected to the front door. He had heard the soft, persistent knocking and gone downstairs to see what it was. Madame was fast asleep. She had taken something, as she often did to help her sleep. She was not a good sleeper.

When he opened the door the children — the girls — were quite visible to him in the moonlight. They were obviously sisters. They must have been about twelve and fifteen years old. They looked very similar, their shaved heads giving them an oriental air. He hesitated to take them in because of his wife, their unborn child. They could only bring trouble, he knew. He knew where they must have come from, after all, and they were probably riddled with lice and disease. They must have been on the road for a while. He led them into the kitchen and put out a loaf of bread and poured some milk into two tin bowls, intending to send them packing as soon as they had eaten. It was then that he noticed the wild, hunted look in their eyes. They were desperate.

He could hardly bear to watch as they tore at the bread with trembling hands and gulped down the milk. Even at such a moment they did not entirely forget their manners but stopped every now and then to glance at him warily and mutter their thanks.

And yet, they were very beautiful too, as only young girls can be, even with their shaved heads and their faces elongated with fever and fatigue, their wild eyes and their soiled, smocked dresses, he said, as his gaze traveled over my face. He stared at me in a way that made me shiver slightly and lower my gaze. "Young people cannot imagine how they look to us: clean, even when they are filthy; dewy, with a sort of sheen — all of them, even the plain ones."

Had Monsieur been heroic after all? Had I been mistaken about him? For a moment I saw him as I wished to see him, as Julien Sorel, as Rodrigue.

In the end he had taken them in, he said, and kept them hidden in the attic. He said he supposed there were Jews hidden all over the place in Europe in those days. Luis was the one who had looked after them, taking them food up there and giving them clean clothes.

I remembered the dress in the bed and the drawing of Luis in the margin of the book, the names, entwined with flowers: Anna and Lea. I imagined them sitting up there in the silence and the heat of the attic and writing to one another so as not to make any noise.

What had made him change his mind, he admitted, was the sound of their voices: these were not gypsy children, not working class. They spoke with the educated tones of children of the bourgeoisie. "Rather like you, in a way," he said, making me think of their writing. I did not mention it, however. The words remained my secret, and theirs.

I wish the gendarme had allowed me to bring Marie France. Why could I not have brought my doll, at least?

How can you be so stupid as to weep over a doll?

It's so boring up here, especially at night. All I can think about is Maman. I wish we could go outside, just for a moment. It's dark enough. No one would see us, would they? I so want to climb a tree. Look at the branches; I feel I can see them grow in the dark. I want to run in the grass. My leg is asleep. It feels dead. And my hands are dying, too. We are dying up here, little by little, day after day. I need at least to move about without being so afraid. Time goes by so slowly.

It is better up here than in the camp, with all those screaming children and the rats.

At least we were all together, there. We were not dependent on strangers bringing us food.

We are lucky to have found someone who would take us in. Just stop complaining.

I wish someone else were here with me, and not you.

They had gone to a local lycée, he was sure, and had learned all the facts those schools manage to cram into French children's heads. Their parents may have been foreigners, but the girls were born in France — that distinction was somehow important to Monsieur. You could see someone had dressed them up at some point with great care. They still wore those long white socks and the shoes with the bars across the top, those childish socks that all the French bourgeois children wear. All they were missing were the shiny plaits with the big white bows.

They had learned French history as he had, starting every school year at the beginning with the Cave Man and going all the way through to the time just before the First World War, over and over again, each time in more and more detail. Not a bad method, actually, for learning something, he remarked and looked at me sharply.

When I woke this morning I thought I was back on the Rue des Rosiers, and I was late for school. I had forgotten to learn my poem by heart, Victor Hugo's poem about his dead daughter, and all I could remember was "Demain, des l'aube, à l'heure," I was so frightened.

How much longer can we just sit and wait up here?

What had happened to them? Was it possible that he would have taken advantage of two helpless children and made love to them as he was making love to me? I looked at him more closely, noticed the lines in the corners of his eyes, around the mouth. For a moment he looked older, tired, sinister. When I asked him what had become of them, he stared across the room in silence, considering. Then he frowned and twitched his shoulders and said he had never been quite sure what had made them leave so suddenly.

"They just left?"

Perhaps they had decided they wanted to make their way back to Paris to find their father, he said.

Why did Papa have to go away?

Because he knew they would pick him up, but he never thought the French would come after women and children. Papa always said they were looking for the important Jews: the Rothschilds, the Blums, not ordinary people like us.

He added, "You gave me a terrible fright when I saw you lying up there in that bed. For a moment, I thought they had come back."

He lay down his napkin by his plate delicately and leaned close to me, whispering, "You want me, don't you? Tell the truth." I felt the flying feeling, as if a rush of air had lifted me just above the floor.

He told the waitress to bring another bottle of sparkling white wine. I chose my favorite dessert, crème brûlée, in a little flat dish with a hard crust of sugar. I could not wait to hold the thick, sweet custard in my mouth, but as I ate I could not help thinking of the young girls' words, words I read and reread in the dust and the heat of the attic, trying to understand them.

You should not have spent all the money on pastries. You spent two hundred francs on pastries!

You were the one who wanted to. You said the first thing you wanted to do was find a pastry shop. You made me go into the pastry shop and spend all our money.

I didn't tell you to spend all the money. You just did!

We will get a reply to our package soon. Papa will come and rescue us.

Just sit quietly and stop bothering me all the time, can't you?

Who else can I bother?

Then I forgot the girls in the attic, I forgot his wife, as he questioned me in detail about my mother, my boarding-school friends, Richard, the doctor I had seen in Paris. He led me on from subject to subject, always reflecting anything I said in a highly flattering way, like one of those mirrors that sends back an enhanced reflection, erasing lines and blemishes.

Did his blue eyes really glimmer with tears, his full lower lip tremble? Yes they did, yes they did. He was telling me I would make him a very happy man if I would consent to come with him on a voyage just now.

"And Madame?" I asked faintly.

He said, "Catherine has her own agenda. She was not born yesterday, you know. She understands how these things happen. She is a wise woman, and she has business of her own in Paris. I have told Luis to keep an eye on her. Besides, we will get you back before she returns, I promise. We will not leave her alone at the mill. I would never do that to her," he promised, stroking my thigh so that my whole body trembled. He added, "I would say we had her blessing, wouldn't you?"

11

WHEN I WAS SEVEN years old and my sister nine, Mother took us to England. We sailed on the *Queen Mary* to Southampton and from there took the train to London. We were told we would see the castle where the queen lived. But when we looked up at the square gray edifice that was Buckingham Palace, we were deeply disappointed.

The castle Monsieur took me to looked the way it was supposed to, like one of the fairy castles in the books of my childhood. In the distance, glimmering white and enchanting, turrets soared in the dawn light. We drove through the iron gates, down the tree-lined driveway, and across the pebbled courtyard, where Monsieur parked the car under the chestnut trees. He took me by the hand and led me across the thick grass of the dew-damp lawn, which made my sandals wet. We went up white marble steps, through glass doors, and across a thin Oriental carpet.

While he arranged for a room, I looked out the big windows at the moat, dry now and mossy, and the drawbridge, permanently lifted. I saw the flags flying in the wind, and in the distance, the wide, capricious river, flowing now fast, now slowly, often overflowing, Monsieur told me, taking me by the hand, carrying off the lives of those who dared to live too close to its banks.

Monsieur led me past a giant blue-and-white bowl of mixed flowers, up the low, wide stairs, and along a quiet corridor to our room. He threw open the long windows onto the soft, delicate light of the Île-de-France.

A great park with lakes surrounded the castle. We ate breakfast there in the sunshine: fresh croissants, fruit, and coffee with frothy milk. Purple bougainvillea tumbled down the terrace, and honeysuckle grew wild along the hedge. The sun came and went behind passing clouds.

Afterward we went back to our room to shower. When I came out of the bathroom, Monsieur was asleep on the wide, canopied bed, half-clothed, his hands folded behind his head. I caught a glimpse of his stomach, the sweep of a thin thigh. His skin was as white as milk and his face motionless as a mask. He looked old, and for a moment I was aware of what I had done, coming here on my own with him. I wanted to shake him awake and beg him to drive me to Paris to my sister and her new baby, but he stirred slightly and opened his eyes and reached out his hand to me, "Come here, *cocotte*," he said tenderly.

By day, we visited one after another of the famous castles: Blois, Chambord, Cheverny, Amboise, Chenonceaux, Loches, Azay-le-Rideau, others whose names I forget. We wandered aimlessly, lazily following the river, moving on whenever I wished from one place to the next. I held the green Michelin guide in my lap and directed Monsieur along the straight roads, the trees arching over us like a bower. With his hands in driving gloves, he held the wooden wheel of his low-slung car. We stopped to picnic on a plaid blanket in some open field on delicacies I chose in the charcuteries: pâté, crudités and *saucisson sec,* ripe cheeses and fresh bread and wine. We ate dinner on the terraces of small inns by starlight.

The weather continued unusually clear and cloudless. It became hotter and heavier as we went farther south, and the summer season advanced, growing sultry and suffused with sloth. We rose late, if I wished; we sauntered along shaded allées in the gardens of the castles or, if I preferred, through the cool, dark halls, while Monsieur answered my questions.

He was better than any guidebook. He knew, or said he knew, the intimate details of the lives of the people who had lived in these castles. He told me wild and wonderful tales of the royal and not so royal who had resided there. I learned about rivalry and murder for passion and power. I heard about the cages where Louis XI had kept his prisoners, too small to stand or lie down in, designed to keep his captives crouching for the rest of their lives. I gazed on the statue of the charming Agnès Sorel, lying with the angels supporting her head and the two lambs to remind us of her name. I heard about the Mistress of Blois who was unable to resist the great seducer the duke of Orléans and kept him supplied with her husband's gold until he was obliged to sell the castle to the duke himself; about Louise de Lorraine, the inconsolable, who mourned her husband for eleven years, wearing white, becoming known as the White Queen; about the assassination of the duc de Guise; about Diane de Poitiers, who rose at six and washed in cold water, rode for three hours in the morning, negotiated with the Protestants, sold Spanish captives, and maintained her vigor to an advanced age; about Louis XVI's sexual problems, the operations he had undergone on his private parts so that he could produce an heir; about his wife, Marie Antoinette, who had appealed to the mothers in the crowd when she faced the women who wanted her life; about Mary Stuart, the foreigner married to Francis II, who died when he was my age. I saw Clouet's portrait of her at Chantilly: the perfect oval face, the fine, straight nose, the big, soft eyes.

We wandered around the small towns shopping, as I had done with Madame, only this time it was I who made the selections. I had Monsieur buy me a tiny black bikini and a pair of gold, dangling earrings and three entwined gold bracelets, like hers, which still jangle when I move my arm to type these words in this quiet room above the city, the rain on my windowpane like tinsel.

Much of the time I would stay in my bathing suit, not bothering to dress. I sauntered naked in the hotel room, gladdening Monsieur's heart. He lay lazily on the bed, lifting his head to watch and reach out to touch me as I went by. I liked his pleasure in me, his natural ability to take pleasure in all its forms. It encouraged me to take satisfaction in the world around me. I would drop my wet suit onto the bathroom floor, pour bath salts liberally into the hot water, and lie there dreaming for hours. My consciousness became veiled by a pleasant mist. I was light and slightly dizzy, as though I were a balloonist floating through the air.

Monsieur gave in to the most capricious of my desires, which became, therefore, increasingly capricious. A noise would bring about a change of room, a meal would be sent back to the kitchen if it were not hot enough, or a bottle of wine, insufficiently cold. He listened to my childish chatter for hours and patiently endured my silences, my shifting moods, my moments of remorse. Every day, at my instigation, he called Madame and spoke to her at some length.

Nights, as I lay in the wide, canopied bed, reading my guidebook in the light of the lamp, he caught me up in his arms, and I felt his heart beat hard. I laughed at him, allowing him to remove my nightclothes. His breath was close against my face. He named every part of my body a different fruit as he gathered it up. My cheeks, my elbows, my knees were ripe peaches and plums, my behind was quince or apple or pear; my breasts were grapefruits, melons; my nipples, raspberries, strawberries, gooseberries, he told me, nibbling on them. He called my dark hidden place the fruit of the vine.

Watching his antics in the pool of light from the lamp, I was unmoved. I felt that I was not obliged to pretend. The fraudulent sighs and little moans copied from films, which I had deemed necessary with Richard, had no place here. Monsieur showed me the still lifes of my body, lit up by his gaze, as though I had never seen them before, like pictures in an exhibition. "Look, look, at this," he said, still playing the guide as he touched the inside of my knee. "See this," he exclaimed as he stroked my clavicle, where the bone lies just beneath the skin. He smoothed the down on my legs, the indent of a dimple in my behind, the stain of a birthmark on my shoulder. "Look how much you resemble my Catherine," he would say.

I imagined Madame lying between us in the white sheets, on her back, her silky legs spread wide with abandon. As he stroked me, her skin turned pink and pearly.

I felt an immense curiosity about the couple's life together. I wanted to know everything. I begged Monsieur to tell me how they had made love for the first time, wondering if he would admit, as she had, about their difficulties. He said he had seen her for the first time in church one Sunday at mass, sitting in the pew next to her old aunt in her flowered hat and mauve gloves. When he looked at Madame now he could still see that little girl — she was a few years younger than he — in a white, smocked dress and plaits, striking poses, peeping over her shoulder slyly. He could not remember a time when they had not been in love. They had made love in forests, in fields, and in the backs of taxis. Madame could not live without him, he knew, that was her weakness, her Achille's heel if you will, but he said his infidelity excited her as well as him. He used it, telling her in detail how he made love to his mistresses. His cheek was on my thigh, his tongue entering me. Caressing me all along the side of my body with his hands and his sex, he told me how he would make her wait until she begged him to take her, getting down on her knees, throwing her head back, her fine hair loose and glossy, her eyes glittering with tears, her upper lip beaded with sweat, groveling abjectly. Now I was slipping from the bed, down, down on my hands and knees, my hair around my shoulders, asking him to take me, please.

Looking at me, he said, "Without me she cannot go on; I will never leave her, you understand, there is no question of that."

Then he gathered me up and pulled me onto the bed and gazed at me with hope, helplessly. He said, "Pretty little thing, you pretty little darling," and he put his cool hands on my neck, and loosened my thick, wild hair, and I shook it from side to side. He whispered, "Your hair, your thick hair," and I saw the light glitter in it, the whirling mass with its reddish sparks like the twilight of the sea. He put his tongue in my mouth. He put his fine hands on my face and stroked my eyelids.

Stop sniffling. I cannot stand the sound of your sniffling anymore.

I keep thinking how Maman slipped us that little piece of soap at the last minute, to make sure we would stay clean.

It doesn't help to sniffle. You have to smile and do as you're told. People don't like sad children. Do you want them to stop bringing us food? Do you want them to send us away? Don't you understand how lucky we are to be here? They could send us back to the camp anytime. They could send us off to Germany, to Poland.

I want to go to Germany to find Maman.

How could those children find their mothers again?

They didn't even know their names, and they had lost their identification numbers.

When my hair has grown back I'm going to run outside and let them send me to Germany. I can't stand to wait up here any longer. I'm going to find Maman, so she can see me with my lovely, long hair again.

How you cried when they cut off your hair! You cried more for your hair than for Maman. Hot tears running down your cheeks. Poor, vain, lovely, little Lea. I, too, miss the light in your long auburn hair.

That horrible gendarme smacked me and said he was going to make me the "Last of the Mohicans!" I can still see his face bent over me, with his red hair and his red mustache. He shoved my head between his knees and traced a line through my hair, and when I put my head up everyone laughed at me. I was so ashamed.

You were not the only one; they did that to a whole bunch of children.

Then he put his sex inside me and I saw the light spinning, a Catherine Wheel. I put my hands on the damp skin of his back as he rose and fell, waves of light and shadow rippling over me. His head blocked the sunlight. Each time he thrust in me I let go of something. I cut the rope, released the boat from its mooring; I left the earth behind. I was gliding out silently into the white glare. I wanted to beg him to remain in me forever, to go on wandering from the turrets of one castle to another. I wanted to keep his seed within me, to bear his children. I wanted to say, don't stop, don't ever stop what you are doing to me.

I was very near to being happy for perhaps the first time in my life. I was soon intoxicated with constant love-making, and spoiled with good living.

All of this made what happened afterwards even more terrible and sad.

12

MONSIEUR LAY ON HIS STOMACH, reaching across to remove the receiver from its cradle on the bedside table. Then he sat up, and I sat on his lap as he spoke. I whispered words of endearment into his ear. After a while, I went downstairs to the pool and swam up and down fast. When I came back, he was still on the telephone, talking in a low voice, using the familiar *tu*, but with a slightly distant tone, as one would to someone inferior or younger. I felt a sudden and inconvenient curiosity about what he had been saying.

He was still in the blue silk pajama top I had chosen for him in some small shop, and the tray from our breakfast lay in the crumpled, sex-stained sheets. I was wearing the tiny black bikini he had bought me, and dripping wet from my swim.

We were in a hotel room in some small French town, visiting an obscure château I had insisted on visiting but whose name I forget. I remember the big, airy room, the white curtains floating, the light-splashed copies of Impressionist paintings, the floral carpet damp from my feet.

I had just seen an acquaintance of my mother's, a large woman with red hair, sitting by the pool, her plump feet up on her chaise longue, her painted pink toenails shining. She had watched me swim. When I pulled myself up out of the water, she stared at me, the sunlight coming through the holes of her straw hat, casting a lace of shade on her face. I could see her thinking, I know that girl from somewhere. I had climbed out of the pool fast and run past her before she could remember where it was.

Now I came over and shook water on Monsieur, my gold bracelets jangling. I kissed him on the mouth, greedily.

"I'm afraid we'll have to pack our things," he said regretfully.

"Right away?" I asked, throwing up my hands, the drops of water falling to the flowers in the carpet pattern.

"Well, yes. We have been away much longer than planned. We have to leave now, if you want to get back home before she does."

I no longer wished to get back before Madame did; I no longer wished to see her again. What I wanted was to continue wandering with Monsieur for the rest of my life. But I moved fast around the room, feeling as if it had suddenly shrunk, as if there were not enough air in there, as if the paintings had lost their luster.

He was going back to her. He had never said he would not, in fact he had always warned me he would, but somehow I had believed otherwise. How could he, who possessed my heart, not want what I wanted? I kept glancing at him, thinking: He is going to change his mind; he is going to say he is joking. But he, too, looked different: hard, poised, decided, not as he had when he had lain in my arms and harvested the fruits of my body.

I turned away and pushed my things into my backpack, pell-mell, leaving in the closet a new sundress with thin straps, which I had worn without much underneath. I said not a word. I banged things about, slamming the cupboard door, the empty drawers. I thought that when he saw my distress he would change his mind. I was used to getting my way with him. But he went on dressing calmly in his orderly fashion, folding back his cuffs, adjusting his cufflinks. He went into the bathroom to collect his toilet articles: his razor, his eau de cologne, the pink salve he borrowed from Madame. He went downstairs to pay the hotel bill.

I locked myself in the bathroom and lay flat on the cold floor, where surely no one else had ever lain. I remembered how he had felt inside me and wept, louder and louder, my cheek against the hard tile. Then I rose and flushed the toilet a few times. My body felt numb. My head was throbbing. I was thinking of my mother's friend, whom I had seen by the pool, of how she had once stood up at a party and sung a tune in a completely flat voice. This memory made me laugh, so that I was laughing and weeping at the same time.

We drove fast without stopping all day. My face was stiff and set, my mouth dry and my legs cramped. My plaited, pinned-up hair had dust in it. I needed to go to the bathroom. I was already missing his body. The wheels murmured, "Don't leave me; don't leave me; don't leave me."

I could not keep from staring at him as he drove, with his dark glasses hiding his light blue eyes, his driving gloves covering the palms of his fine hands, his collar beating in the wind; his skin shimmering like milk, masklike, in the sun. Oblivious to me, he concentrated entirely on the road.

So often in life, unlike in literature, we are unable to remember precisely a moment of change. Our perception shifts gradually over time. It is rather like someone who wakens in bed without knowing the precise moment of awakening. But that day in the car, I remember clearly understanding for the first time what had happened to me. I had no key to this man. I knew nothing about his life away from me. Much of him remained like the uncut pages of a book.

I realized then that I was not so much in love with him as in thrall to him, to Madame, to their mill, their language, their literature, their history, their country's beauty. They had inundated me; they were part of me. I was without any other desire. I had no thought for the future or the past. Carelessly, recklessly, I did not consider anything but the present and those freckles on his broad, strong back. There was no doubt in my mind, though, perhaps there had never been since I first read that sentence in the book in their attic, that the situation was extremely dangerous. I knew, I believe, even then, that all of this could end only badly.

The sudden withdrawal of Monsieur's favor left me with longing. Making love to him, I had seen the world bright and clear, but now it was blurring. I was sinking into a dim, dusky region, a place of moths, bats, and darkness.

My eyes filled with tears. I could hardly see where we were going: the trees and sky grew dark. Misery was there. I could almost touch it.

The dog ran out joyfully to greet us in the half dark. He jumped all over me, licking my face with passion. Monsieur dragged his small black leather suitcase out of the trunk and went into the house. I was left with my heavy backpack to listen to Dolores's endless complaints: her pains, her crossed intestines, her longing for her Luis, her concern for Madame, who was still in Paris, who had been away all this time. All I could do was crouch down and hug the excited dog.

As soon as I was able to escape Dolores, I set out after Monsieur, with the dog trailing behind me. I had never ventured into Monsieur's room before, but this time I went up the steps and stood leaning against his door with the dog beside me, my hands folded on my misery, carrying it like a chalice. He was sitting before a desk in a swivel chair with his back to the door. He swung around sharply, the chair creaking. The room was smaller than Madame's, darker and cluttered with heavy furniture: the desk and chair, a daybed, a standing mirror, all gilded and scrolled, from the Napoleonic period. Green paint darkened the walls, and baize topped the large, pompous desk. The *tôle* lamp cast a pool of green light. Thick, dusty velvet curtains closed out the night.

Monsieur had already showered and changed into a clean, white shirt, the sleeves rolled up. He must have shaved and cut his chin; I saw a dot of blood. His wet hair was slicked back neatly from his forehead. He peered at me over his thick tortoiseshell glasses, one eyebrow raised in inquiry, as though he did not quite recognize me, or anyway could see no reason for my presence in his room. It was the old blue shortsighted stare, made even more impersonal through the reading glasses, which, like Madame, he usually avoided out of vanity. He held a glinting silver letter opener in his hand. He was going through his pile of letters.

He remonstrated, "Sweetheart, not here, please, not in my room," as though I were a dog who had misbehaved. He turned back to his letters, slitting open another envelope, the sound of it ripping my heart.

He half-turned so that I could see him in profile, the nose long and sharp. He cleared his throat and spoke dispassionately, and even, I thought, with a certain relief, as though this were something he had wanted to say for a while. "My dear Dodo," he began, with dignity, his words clipped, saying something about all good things coming to an end. "Take the dog out of here and go back to your room like a good girl," and he touched the cut on his chin with the tips of his fingers. Then he turned his back on me.

I could feel him waiting for me to go. His shoulders twitched with impatience. I thought, If you don't move now, you will never be able to. He will have you dragged away. He will call Dolores and she will come and carry you down the stairs.

I am too tired, too tired, I thought, but I dragged myself from his doorway and down the stairs, past the pugilists with their raised fists, and across the wide, half-empty salon with its round window staring down at me menacingly. I went up the slippery stairs to my old room with its narrow bed, lumpy bolster, and peeling green wall linen.

I remembered his coming to me the night of the party: "Why struggle against passion? Is it not the most beautiful thing in the world? Is it not the source of everything lovely? Of art and song?" I thought of Madame's visit the next morning. "Why don't you talk this over with Guy?" It all seemed to have happened a long time ago.

I climbed the stairs to the bathroom and stood before the mirror over the basin, looking at my pale face, my red-rimmed eyes, my drooping mouth, my dusty hair. My face had changed from round and hopeful to angular and sad. There was something severe in my brow now. Could loving make you so ugly? Yes it could, it could.

13

DOLORES RAN TO THE WINDOW at the sound of each passing car. It was past noon, and Madame had still not arrived. Dolores kept saying, "I hope all is well. I hope nothing bad has happened to Madame." Naturally, she was waiting not only for Madame but for her Luis, too, who had been absent the whole time, driving Madame around Paris. Madame's promised few days had turned into several weeks. Finally, the black Citroën appeared at the top of the driveway. The wind flapping her voluminous skirts around her short, fat legs, Dolores, followed by the dog, ran out wildly into the courtyard to greet Madame and Luis. Madame knelt down to embrace the dog as Monsieur strolled casually across the pebbled courtyard in his scuffed moccasins. He wore his navy sweater, slung around his shoulders and knotted on his chest, keeping one hand in the pocket of his rumpled linen pants.

He shook Luis's hand, bent his head toward him, and spoke to him briefly, while Luis grinned up at him boyishly, displaying all his white teeth. Then, Monsieur embraced his wife in the French fashion, left cheek, right cheek, left cheek. As though nothing had happened, he slung his arm around her shoulder and brought her slowly back into the house, lowering his head toward her, talking and laughing.

Dolores had polished the furniture to a high shine that morning, and I had arranged the late-blooming roses in a bowl. Everything had seemed to glow, but when Monsieur and Madame had entered the room, though it was early afternoon and still late summer, things grew misty, smoky, and damp. I shivered. Hunters' guns sounded in the distance. The autumn shooting had begun in earnest.

What had I expected to happen? I had forgotten what seemed to me the couple's fatal similarity: those identical light blue shortsighted eyes, the full, knowing lips, the high white foreheads. They were even wearing the same colors: Monsieur in navy blue pants and sweater with a white shirt and Madame in a narrow navy skirt and white silk blouse.

They had been pledged to one another by their parents before they were born; their union was inevitable, indissoluble, I thought. Their shared history went back into the beginnings of their nation. They had learned all the arts; they were wise and perspicacious and cruel. They knew about people, and they exploited them.

Madame embraced me warmly, and I smelled her cloying lily-scented perfume, the one she had bought for me as well. She kissed me on both my cheeks, and later I found the traces of the vivid pink lipstick there, like the marks from the slap of a hand. She said she was delighted to find her little guest still there. She looked around the room and remarked on the roses I had cut and placed on the mantel-piece. She pulled me toward her, and I felt her soft, comforting body against mine. For a moment, I wanted to weep on her shoulder, to ask her to comfort me; then I drew back from her, my body stiff with misery.

She seemed rested, cheerful, full of enthusiasm and new energy. She at once took her household back into her capable hands. She had Dolores rearrange the dishes in the big cupboard in the pantry. She sent Luis off to clean out the garage. Her little hands were in constant motion, adjusting her perfectly smooth hair, her impeccable blouse.

She invited me for a walk across the fields before dinner, and I accompanied her in sullen silence. She floated fast across those flat, dry fields beside me, a pale blue scarf tied tightly around her neat head. The wheat had been cut and tied in great stacks by then. The dog, who had doubtless been kept tied up by Dolores during our absence, bolted ahead of us, and we had to call him back repeatedly.

Madame asked me about the different châteaux we had visited. I answered briefly, listing the castles as though reciting something out of a guidebook. "I knew you and Guy would sort things out," she said with a sly sideways glance at me. She linked her arm with mine in a conspiratorial fashion, as though we were all joined together now. I thought dully of the wives in a harem giggling shamelessly.

I recalled how she had riveted her gaze on Monsieur on her return. I imagined them together in her big, sunny bedroom taking breakfast in bed. They were laughing about me. "Oh, you naughty, naughty boy," Madame was saying and he, "To tell you the truth, I'm getting too old for this sort of thing."

Madame told me, her cheeks flushing, that she, too, had had a most successful visit. She had shopped, visited the exhibitions, attended the theater. She had seen many of her friends. She confessed she had found a new psychiatrist, who was actually related to one of her friends — such a charming man, so elegant and from such an old family, my child. Their families were even vaguely connected on the distaff side.

Everyone in her world was connected, even the shrinks, I thought bitterly. Someone was always there to introduce her to someone else, someone who might help. This one had been most helpful, most helpful, she maintained.

"What a clever man," she said. This was the first time I had heard of her visits to people of this profession, and I looked at her with some surprise. I gathered from what she said that there had been a string of unsuccessful treatments before this one.

"Of course, he was terribly expensive. An elegant office just off the Avenue Foch," she exclaimed, waving her small hands to indicate something large. "And I liked the man so much, when I had got over the way he looked," she commented.

"How did he look?" I asked.

"Not a hair on his head." She laughed and added, "Yul Brynner in person." Then she pulled at a blade of long grass and took a more serious tone and went on. "But he is obviously very brilliant. Suicide seems to be his specialty. I noticed heaps of books on the subject. He had so many books in his consulting rooms. He lent me one by someone called Durkheim. Looked frightfully dull to me, and I didn't read it, of course, but perhaps you would like to?"

"Perhaps I will," I said and glanced at her.

"And he was amazingly nice. Saw him every day. Talked all the time. Talked more about himself than me, actually, which was a relief, if you know what I mean?" She laughed a little, and I realized she was staring inquisitively at me.

I laughed nervously. I had difficulty concentrating on her story. I was wondering if she had noticed the absence of her cameo, or if she had forgotten about it. She did not mention it but instead squeezed my hand and said, "Don't tell Monsieur about the new psychiatrist, will you? He doesn't know I have been seeing anyone new. He thinks I'm still seeing that awful old doctor in Pithiviers, whom I have been seeing for years. Never did me any good. I don't think he has ever said a word except to tell me to eat and get some exercise. You know how Guy feels about that sort of thing. He doesn't even like me to get a massage. Oddly enough, he's a very jealous man, is he not?"

"Is he?" I said, and thought of Monsieur's words in Estouy: "I don't want you seeing him again."

"The only difficulty was Luis: his driving gets worse and worse, and the constant grumbling. He didn't like being in Paris, at all. He didn't want to take me out at night — naturally, I saw a few old beaux — he had the audacity to tell me it was dangerous. He complained about his lodgings, the rudeness of the Parisians, the traffic. Honestly, that man will be the death of me. If only I could think of some pretext to get rid of him. It would be easier to drive the car myself. I'm thinking about it, to tell you the truth."

At dinner, Madame sat erect at one end of the table in a new white dress with a necklace of lapis lazuli around her pale neck. The windows were open, and the bright daisies shook in the evening wind.

Monsieur sat at the other end, and in the candlelight they ate and talked. I recalled my first dinner in that house when Madame had pushed her peas around her plate, sighing, and Monsieur had sat in sullen silence. Tonight they gossiped about Madame de Signé, I believe she was called, anyway some woman who had come to their wedding in an absurd hat, which she had made herself, or perhaps it was her dress that was absurd. Madame had bumped into her in Paris. Like teenagers the couple giggled over the poor lady.

Are they really so beautiful? I thought. No, they are not. They are really not beautiful at all, their full lips shiny with grease, their mocking faces distorted. They are self-possessed and superficial, with a harsh rakishness I had never noticed before.

Is theirs a love affair? No, theirs is a fight to the death.

Monsieur glanced at my untouched plate and remonstrated: "We don't want to have to pay for a doctor now, do we?" I scowled back at him, and even considered telling him about Madame's new doctor, but instead took a mouthful of Dolores's delicious stew. It stuck in my throat, and bitter steam rose from the dish.

I took on a superior, pretentious air and talked about Sartre and Simone de Beauvoir: "There is really no reason why we should not share everything we have. What is wrong with socialism?"

Madame smiled and said, hardly glancing at me, "We have a saying in French, 'The heart to the left but the wallet to the right.'"

I listened to the sound of the wind and the endlessly running water, and picked up my knife, tracing patterns on the tablecloth with the tip, glancing from her to him. I was not quite sure which one I wanted more to kill.

They excused themselves, saying they were tired, as they had done the first night I was with them. But this time, as they climbed the stairs, I heard the sound of their laughter mingling harmoniously, the same chord played in different octaves. While I remained at the table, stirring and stirring a bitter cup of black coffee, I heard unmistakable giggles followed by soft moans.

Did they know I was listening to them? Yes, they did, they did, and my pain added to their pleasure.

I retreated to my narrow bed to toss and turn, my body burning as if I had a fever. I rose finally and climbed back up the stairs into the attic, as I had done so many times before. This time I was not wandering aimlessly; I knew what I was looking for.

I settled myself in the bed up there, closed the stiff velvet bed curtain, and lit the lamp. This time I read with resolve and puzzled over each entry carefully. I discovered ones I had never seen before in unexpected corners and small spaces. I forced myself to read over the words in the margins, comprehending some of them for the first time. I studied the drawing of Luis: the features that I now knew so well. One of the girls had captured his narrow face, his foxlike expression, his pompous air. I wondered at his role in their unfolding drama.

How unfair that the little children called someone else Maman.

Did they?

Don't you remember how they would just call out to any other woman who went by, "Maman! Maman!" It seems so cruel. Think of their poor mothers. They must be so unhappy, and they do not even know that their children are calling someone else Maman.

Who knows what has happened to their mothers, to Maman.

Who knows what will happen to us.

Why do the Germans hate us so?

I wonder why the gendarme allowed me to go and buy a comb for Maman. The woman in the shop told me not to go back to the apartment. "Don't go back, don't go back," she kept saying. "Run away, child!"

You should have run away.

But where would I have gone? How could I leave Maman and you?

I keep thinking of how I told Maman I didn't want to sleep with her because her straw was all wet. How could I have refused to sleep beside her that last night? If only I had known it would be for the last time.

Don't say it was for the last time, please. Don't say that!

Soon we will get some response, surely, and we'll be able to leave here and go back to Paris. Surely Papa will get the package and the jewelry. It must be worth something. He'll come and save us.

Don't worry, Lea, I'm going to take care of you. I promise we'll never have to get on that train again, no matter what happens.

I feel so stiff from sitting here for so long, waiting and waiting.

As long as you can see the blue sky out of the window and hear the sound of the water, how can you be so sad?

It's boring, boring, boring, and I miss Maman so.

Just keep quiet. We are better here than in Germany.

What if someone finds us up here. What if the police come and find us?

Other entries now interested me. This was one:

Freckles, he has freckles on his back.

Do you think he will bring us a reply tonight? Surely Papa must have received our package by now.

They won't find us if you are quiet enough and stop fidgeting and coughing. Can't you control yourself?

I wish I could have hidden in this attic with someone else, anyone else! I hate you. I hate you. I hate the way you smell when you have been with him.

Keep quiet. I keep telling you to lie quietly. Don't you understand what will happen to us if they find us? Don't you see that I have to do what he asks me to do?

Will they shoot us?

They will send us to Germany, and we will be murdered.

Why would they murder us? Why would anyone murder children?

Maman's friend said they were gassing all the Jews. She heard it on the radio.

Is gassing a quick way to die? Do you suppose when you die it's like suffocating slowly, like when you hold your breath or go underwater?

I don't want to die! Just stay quietly on the bed and do as you are told to do, and no one will find us.

I began to realize what the American professor, William Hawthorne, had been trying to tell me. I imagined the searchers coming into the camp to look for valuables, slitting open eiderdowns, pillows, forcing the women down onto the floor, examining their most intimate places. I imagined the jewels floating in the latrines among the white worms as big as fingers in the feces. I saw the money the Jews had ripped up before they left floating through the air like dust, landing on the lawn.

I saw the scenes of separation: the children torn from their mothers, who beat their heads against the walls, against the earth, before they were dragged away and left to stand all day, their hands on the barbed wire, watching their children, calling to them on the other side. I saw the policemen forcing the women up into the packed cattle cars.

I imagined the camp, the thousands of abandoned children wandering back and forth, snotty-nosed, diapers on backwards, diarrhea dribbling down their legs, calling any adult Maman, or sitting in silence, unable to smile, unable to speak, unable to remember even their own names.

This time I took the book back with me to my room and slipped it into my drawer.

I remembered losing my own mother once in a crowded street on holiday at the shore. I must have been five or six. It was only a moment, but I remembered that terrible fear of abandonment, and I wept, the hot tears running down my cheeks. What did my unhappiness matter beside all of this? It did not matter at all. Still, I might not have acted as I did if I had not spoken to Cecile.

14

ONSIEUR AND MADAME had gone to a dinner party at the château, he in his smoking jacket and white silk scarf, she in black chiffon with glittering sequins all over the bodice. There had been no question of my accompanying them. I had opened a bottle of Monsieur's heavy red wine and already helped myself to several glasses when the telephone rang. It was the American woman, Mary Hawthorne, calling from the château. She spoke in a low voice. "We had hoped you would join us this evening, dear," she said.

"I didn't know I was invited," I replied, surprised by the kindness of her call.

"But yes. We have been thinking about you, William and I. We were rather worried." She paused.

I did not know what to say, standing in the hall staring down at my bare feet.

"Is everything all right, dear? We heard, you know, that . . ." She paused again. "That you and Guy had gone away."

"I visited some of the châteaux in the Loire valley," I said, trying to keep my voice steady, undone by her concern.

"I see. Well, please let us know how you are. Stay in touch, will you? If you should need something?"

"Thank you so much," I stammered.

"Perhaps a call to your family? Your sister in Paris? Would that be a good idea?"

"Thank you for thinking of me," I said, my cheeks wet as I hung up the phone.

I blew my nose, poured myself another glass of wine, and stole a thick portion of overripe Brie from the refrigerator. I ate the cheese with a tomato on half a baguette at the kitchen table with the dog sitting bolt upright, all attention, by my side. I gave him a big piece, too. The dog loved cheese. Then I telephoned Cecile in Paris.

She said, "I'm so glad you finally called, Dodo. I tried to reach you several times, but some woman with a heavy accent said you were away visiting the châteaux. When are you coming back to us?"

"Thought I was not wanted," I replied, adopting an injured tone.

"Oh, Dodo, don't be so silly. Water under the bridge. I'm sorry. Jean Luc may have overreacted, and I was so preoccupied with my pregnancy. You have to forgive us."

"How are you? How is my namesake?" I asked.

"Baby's fine, but I am feeling awfully blue, to tell you the truth. So lonely for someone from *my* family, and Mother says she's not up to the trip right now," Cecile replied. She told me a long story about her mother-in-law, who was driving her crazy by saying that she did not hold the baby right. "What could be worse!" she exclaimed.

I did not attempt to tell her. Should she not be comforting me? Was I not the one to have lost the baby?

"Where is Mother? How is she? I've had no news at all," I said, my voice starting to quaver again.

"She's gone to that health farm in the Cape to dry out. She tells me she's on the wagon."

"You know what she does down there — bribes the doorman to bring her some booze," I said.

My sister laughed. "I'd love to see you, darling. No one else can make me giggle. Baby keeps me up all night."

"Doesn't Jean Luc help?" I asked, feeling nastier and nastier. I suddenly remembered Cecile once falling upon me and biting me on my back in the garden under the oak tree near the dripping tap where the narcissi grew in the spring.

"Hardly ever here," she said, blowing her nose. I imagined her with her baby at her side, her lovely dark eyes swollen, her snub, freckled nose red. She added, "Naturally, with his patients and all, he can't."

"Look, I don't have any money to make the trip, none at all. That's why I called."

"How is that possible? Mother told me she had sent lots of money down there for your eighteenth. I told her you were blue, and she said she had sent a fortune; enough for a gala, enough to feed an army, and for anything else you might need."

I wondered how much Monsieur and Madame had pocketed after all.

"I'll wire you some money immediately," she promised.

"Good," I said abruptly, already making plans.

"Also, you know, Richard called and called," she added in a lower voice.

"I know. He said you refused to give him my number."

"Yes, well, I thought it might be wiser under the circumstances. And then I was imagining you having a whale of a time visiting all the châteaux with some handsome — "

I interrupted. "I'll come just as soon as my time is up. They are used to having me around."

Cecile adopted an indignant tone, which rather amused me. "I don't see why that should concern you. Look, you're not their bloody servant, after all. I think these people may just be taking advantage of your good nature. You're much too good to them. I'm beginning to think we made a big mistake; the baroness sounded charming on the phone, but who do they think they are? They are supposed to be looking after you! We paid them enough money to look after you. I'd like to give them a piece of my mind."

I tried to imagine anyone giving the de C's a piece of her mind.

"I have some things to settle with them before I leave," I added.

Cecile said, "But, Dodo, surely your own family is more important to you than strangers?"

I said, "You didn't seem so worried about me *before*, if you don't mind my saying so. You seem to be forgetting, *you* were the ones who sent me away."

There was a moment of stunned silence. I could imagine her thinking, Is this my little sister speaking?

Then Cecile said, "Jean Luc just thought a change of air would do you good after what you had been through. You had been lying in our spare room with your face to the wall for just too long. He was worried about you. He thought you were depressed — really — and he thought that it would be better for you to get away. He said women did sometimes get depressed after . . ."

I said, "Jean Luc says a lot of things," remembering how he had said to me, "It's quite simple, really, just a little letting in of air," as though he'd been reading *Hills Like White Elephants*. I wondered how he would have thought it was if he were about to undergo the operation himself.

He had taken me to the doctor's house under cover of night, pushing open the heavy iron gate with his shoulder in the fading light and looking around nervously as he rushed me inside and disappeared fast.

I heard the gate close behind me with a click. The clipped, conical shrubs stood like a row of dark green sentinels before the sandstone house in the *seizième arrondissement*. A maid in a loose blue uniform let me inside. I can still see her sauntering ahead of me down the corridor, her hips swaying, her shapely legs visible in the half-light. A mahogany grand piano shone in the salon, and the doctor's cherubs and his wife stared down at me from silver-framed photographs on the Louis XV mantelpiece, their faces, lit from behind, looking luminous and lovely.

The doctor ushered me into his large office and told me to remove my dress and put my feet up into the steel stirrups on his table. It seemed reasonable enough, and anyway, one always follows doctor's orders, does one not? But this one, when he had me supine and strapped, my petticoat hitched up my thighs, my knees wide, my parts exposed to his probing fingers, decided he would expose his, too, and would take advantage of the interesting situation. "What earthly difference could it make to you now?" he asked, grinning. Afterward, his demeanor altered as he went about the procedure grimly. I was determined I was not going to give him the satisfaction of hearing me scream.

But later that night, rushed to the clinic in pain, my life seeping from me, I lay on a cot in a passageway screaming, and even screaming, I could hear in the distance a baby crying. It was a square brick house in Neuilly with green shutters and roses climbing up the walls and the sound of crows crying in the long, thin cypress in the garden. There was an empty crib in the corridor that I would never forget, for when I looked into it I could see the place where the warm baby's body had been lying. The *sage-femme* who finished the curettage had cold, dry hands and looked down at me disapprovingly when I screamed for something for the pain. "This way, next time, you won't be so careless," she said.

Now I looked out the window at the willows along the river blowing in the night wind. I could hardly remember how Richard's voice sounded or hear the rustle of his blue raincoat. Instead of the lines of his broad, brown face, what came to me were the grave, pale faces and the shaven heads of the children in the attic. I saw the horror of their days etched into their skin like stigmata.

I said to Cecile, "What really rankles is how you and Jean Luc could have told these strangers what happened to me."

She exclaimed indignantly, "But we never told them anything! All I said was that you wanted to be in a family where everyone spoke French. She asked your age, and if you could pay for the stay, and if I had a photograph to send her."

"And you sent her one?"

"Yes — an old one I had knocking about. We must have been about twelve and fourteen, both of us in our school tunics and ties and panama hats."

I exclaimed, "But they knew everything! They knew I had had an abortion, and all about Richard. Perhaps Jean Luc spoke to them without your knowing?"

She said, "Jean Luc may have his faults, Dodo, but can you really imagine him calling up people he admires — a Résistance hero, a baron, with the Légion d'Honneur or whatever, to tell him something unfavorable about his own family? He considers you part of his family, and as far as the outside world goes, his family is just perfect. Did they *tell* you that we had told them about the . . . ?"

"Well, not exactly, but how else could they have found out?"

"I don't know, Dodo, but they sound like they might be the snoopy type. They might have read your diary or one of your letters or something."

I said, "I don't keep a diary, and how could they have read a letter?" but as I said it, I thought of the letter I had written to Mother on my first morning in the de C's house.

15

THE DAY I RECEIVED Cecile's wire with the money, I walked across the courtyard in the sunlight, listening to my sandals slap on the hard, white pebbles, one hand in my pocket feeling for the thick wad of bills. Cecile had made sure the messenger put them into *my* hands this time. I knocked on the door of Dolores and Luis's cottage and waited in the dead quiet and the mid-morning sunlight, listening to the sluggish seeping of the river. Reduced by endless days of summer drought and the increasing pollution, it seemed dead, hardly a river any longer, more a thin ribbon, flecked with the silver sequins of dead fish. Dolores's stained washing dried on a towel horse in the sun, and the cellar door gaped on the dark hole where the bottles of wine were kept.

I watched through a pane of glass in the front door as Dolores shuffled slowly down the narrow, dark stairs in her red dressing gown and flat slippers, clutching her stomach. She had had her period at ten years old, and it had always been extremely painful because of her crossed intestines, the blood being blocked in some mysterious

way, she had explained during one of her breakfast mono-
logues. Now, in the middle age, she was suffering from
symptoms due to the change of life, she had explained at
length. She opened the door, groaning, and led me into the
dark, low-ceilinged cottage, which smelled dank and musty.
She asked me hopefully, squinting and clasping her hands,
if anything were wrong. I said, "I am looking for Luis."

"*Mon* Luis went to Estouy to buy some medicine for me,"
she told me and groaned again, remembering her pains. "But
come in, come in," she urged. "Let me show you around."

She insisted on showing me every nook and cranny of
her small abode, as though it were a famous castle. I was
even called upon to admire the minuscule water closet with
a sink and a hole in the floor and a dangling chain that she
called her bathroom. Perhaps she noticed the expression on
my face, because she said, "Madame is going to install a
proper shower soon."

The place was, miraculously, perfectly clean and tidy.
Snow white crocheted antimacassars covered the arms of
the chairs, embroidered maxims in bright colors hung on
the walls, and useless bronze objects cluttered low, well-
polished tables. A framed photo of Luis and Monsieur took
pride of place over the mantelpiece. His sunken chest bare,
his dark eyes shining with admiration, Luis grinned up at
Monsieur, who stood beside him in an undershirt and
shorts and his bare feet. They both held up some kind of
fish, which I presume they had caught in the days when fish
could still be caught in the river.

When I had duly admired her abode, she sank into an

armchair pathetically and clutched her stomach and would have given me all the details again, but I left before she could ask me why I was looking for her Luis.

I entered the dimly lit back room of the general store in Estouy and looked around for him. As Dolores had predicted, he was there, but he was not buying medicine for his wife's mysterious pains. He was sitting, slumped over slightly in his tight black suit, his hair plastered neatly across his forehead, at a table near the stone wall with a glass of red wine before him.

I stood against the wall and hesitated, wondering if I should disturb him, and if it were wise to ask him anything at all. A small man and narrow-shouldered in his tight black clothes, he seemed to have something sinister, something of the fox, about his face. Perhaps it would be prudent to retreat.

Then, as so often happens, Luis seemed to feel my gaze on him and looked up across the room to where I stood. Startled, he rose fast, smiling somewhat sheepishly and twirling his velvety mustache between finger and thumb before he regained his habitual composure, limping over to me, softly, carefully, looking at me solemnly and bowing his head, explaining gravely that he was taking a moment of rest from his onerous duties, and asking if he could have the honor of offering me a glass of wine. He pulled out a chair for me opposite him, inclining slightly.

I sat down against the wall and put my elbows on the table and folded my hands, facing him. I looked at him directly. I told him I wanted to know something — information he had offered me once, and I had declined. Now I was willing to go so far as to pay for it, if necessary.

He smiled slowly and slyly, and his dark, handsome eyes turned bright. He curled his mustache again and spoke in his pleasant voice, saying that he would be most happy to oblige, that he was not an educated man, but that he knew what was going on in that house; servants usually did. "Does it concern Madame's visit to Paris?" he asked.

"In a way," I answered. I looked around the dimly lit room: the ancient stone walls, the pool table, the blackened beams, the men in their blue overalls. I remembered how Dolores had said she would kill her Luis if he were unfaithful to her, demonstrating her method with a wringing gesture. I even glanced toward the door nervously, remembering how the baron had found me here that day with Richard. I nodded at Luis and slipped some money under the wineglass on the table, but he shook his head and said, "That's not necessary, Mademoiselle."

He smiled at me, all his large, white teeth showing, and told me in his honeyed voice how much he had always liked me, and how he had realized I must have had a difficult time in that house, so far away from my home, my family. He shook his head and clucked his tongue disapprovingly. He lay his hand on his heart and confided that he was a religious man, a believer, a Christian. He leaned forward a little and said that he would be most glad to help me, if he could, in any way. He maintained that he and Dolores had always preferred me to all the other paying guests, that I was obviously from a much better family than most of them, he could see that, he vowed, waving his fine fingers in the air, and then he reached out with one of his swift, delicate gestures, like a bird swooping down for a crumb, and picked up the bills beneath the wineglass and said if I insisted, he could not be so ungracious as to refuse. He lifted his narrow hips ever so slightly and slipped the bills into the pocket of his elegant pants.

He turned his head and looked out the small, dirty panes of the window and sighed and said he and Dolores hoped to return to their home in Spain someday soon. They had already bought a lovely piece of land in the village where they were born, on the side of a hill with a view of the sea. They were saving up to build a house there, a real house just for them, with a proper bathroom, where they could retire, away from all that had happened here. It was their dream.

"I understand," I said and felt moved to slip a few more bills under his glass.

Luis looked down at the table gravely and added that he knew, too, that Monsieur liked me much more than he did most of the previous paying guests. He looked into my eyes directly for a moment in a slightly puzzled way, as if he were trying to see why. I understood that it would not be just money that would make him talk but what he perceived as Monsieur's favor. My luster, if I had any, was reflected.

I lowered my gaze and said that what I wanted to ask him about was a letter I had sent to my mother. He said, "Well, I do know Madame sometimes *looks over* the letters from the paying guests. It is important for her to know what is going on with them. She says that *her* letters were always censored by the nuns in the convent when she was a girl."

"But does she sometimes actually destroy the letters?" I asked.

He looked at me for a moment and then around the room and shifted in his seat. I added a bill, which he slipped into his pocket with an appreciative grin, muttering something about its being far too much, and pushing his dark hair out of his face. He said, "Well, of course, I can't say for certain, but it is possible that if Madame feels the letter would upset the parents too much, she might tear it up. Sometimes things are better left unsaid. No need to upset people unduly, after all, is it not so?"

"That's certainly true," I said.

"She has a tender heart, Madame, you understand, and she worries. She takes her charges very seriously, you see. She's always very worried something might happen to them."

I said, "I see," and added, "So it may have been that a letter I sent to Mother was not actually posted?"

Luis said, "Well, it is possible. On the other hand, it is possible the letter went astray, going all the way to Africa, after all — that is, if your mother never received it. Did your mother not receive it?"

"So she sometimes destroys letters," I said and added, "Might she have done the same with the letters of the two Jewish children who came to the house during the war?"

Luis glanced around the room and leaned toward me and asked me in a whisper who had told me about the girls, and when I said it was Monsieur, he looked chagrined and said, "He told you that? I'm surprised he would tell you that." His shoulders slumped, and he shook his head and sighed and said he did not like to talk about the war. He would rather forget all of that. It would be better for everyone concerned, he felt, not to talk about it, and he glanced sharply at me.

We sipped the red wine, and he looked at me again, and said in a low voice that he himself had taken the girls up to the attic. It was he who had taken care of them, who had brought food and clothing up there for them.

"But how did they escape from the camp? Did they tell you?" I asked. He spoke at some length about them. He seemed to know more than Monsieur had, or was, anyway, willing to tell me more, inspired, perhaps, by my largesse. Or did he have other reasons for telling me what he did? As it was he who had taken care of them, they had confided in him, naturally, he said.

They had worn a double layer of clothing: two dresses each, two pairs of socks, and they had dug under the barbed wire between the two watchtowers at the hour when the guards were most occupied, the hour of the most confusion in the camp: midday, while the guards were giving out the soup. Since the parents had been taken away, the guards had not watched as carefully as they had before. The girls had a little money, sewn into their clothes by their mother before she left on the train, but they had spent it all foolishly, the very first day, in a pastry shop. They were just children, after all. He supposed they were incapable of resisting, stuffing themselves with the pastries they had dreamed about ever since they had been woken in their beds early that Sunday morning in Paris.

"They were picked up in Paris?" I asked.

The gendarmes had come early to their apartment that day. They were fast asleep. They lived on the Rue des Rosiers. Luis said he remembered the address.

"You have a good memory," I remarked, and he smiled modestly and lowered his gaze.

The gendarmes had woken them by beating on the door. Their mother, who had looked out the window — they lived on the fourth or fifth floor — and seen the French police, had reassured them that nothing bad could happen while they were in France. She had not hesitated to open the door. The first thing the gendarmes did when they entered the apartment was close the windows to prevent jumping, as some others had already done.

Luis recounted that the girls had told him many stories when he brought them food at night. He remembered one about them going from house to house, knocking on doors, asking for help. One woman had said she would, but her daughter was ill with the measles. "Oh, but we don't mind," the girls had said, but the woman had declined, saying she would have it on her conscience. Monsieur was the first person to have the kindness to take them in and give them bread.

"How did Monsieur keep them hidden from Madame?" I asked, feeling my face flame with the wine and the words.

"He said it was safer for us to keep it a secret. We told them to be very quiet, especially during the day when people were about, not even to talk."

I leaned across the table and asked him, "But you think she found them?" He was silent for a while, just drumming his fingers on the table. A fly buzzed against the window. Someone shouted out something. The pool balls clicked.

Luis looked at me and seemed to consider the question. "Better not to ask too many questions, Mademoiselle," he warned and shook his head.

But there was no stopping me now. I put my hand into my pocket and felt the cameo on its black ribbon there. I pulled it out and lifted it up and let it dangle back and forth in the air. "Who did this belong to? One of the girls, wasn't it? Did Madame steal it from them?" I asked him. His eyes turned dark and his olive skin, pale.

He said nothing, glancing at me with his crafty eyes.

*Do you think I will live until my birthday? Do you think
I will ever turn twelve and get my period and get a
boyfriend?*

*If you can keep quiet for long enough and stop bother-
ing me.*

*Do you remember how Papa used to tease you when
you first got bosoms?*

"You think Madame suspected something?" I said and felt a sort of flame leap inside me and remembered the words I had read:

Do you think the B. will come again tonight?

*If he does, you must not be such a baby. You must do
what he asks you to do if you want us to be safe in this
place.*

"Anyone might have. There was the extra milk, the bread. Food was scarce at the time, Mademoiselle. We were better off in the country, but still. And it was dangerous to keep people of that sort in the house for any period of time. People denounced one another, you see. Anyone who had a grudge might denounce his enemy, or his rival, to the police. I didn't like it myself, to tell you the truth. I even told Monsieur, I didn't like it. As foreigners, our own position was very precarious, you have to understand. There were very few jobs available, and the French didn't want any more foreigners in their country. You have to comprehend the kind of fear we all lived in at that time. We were protected, fortunately, because we were Spanish, and, of course, we had worked for a long time for the baron, but still. Dolores was always going on about it. You can imagine. It was generous of Monsieur and brave but, after all, there were other people to think of. Madame was expecting a baby herself. She was not well. She has always been fragile. She had already miscarried several times. There had been scares of other kinds. It is possible that she put two and two together."

He, himself, certainly did not wish those girls any harm. He wasn't a racist, had nothing against Jewish people. They stuck together, of course, helped one another and somehow ended up richer than everyone else, but these two, he had to admit, were a better class of Jew than usual. They were educated girls, who spoke very good French and were always very polite to him, he had to say, always thanking him when he brought them anything, asking if they could do anything for him, any mending, sewing. They would have mended his clothes, only Dolores would not have liked that. Of course they depended on him. You might say he protected them and anyway, did what he could.

After the war, no one accused Madame, he went on. People around here did talk about the de C's after the liberation, because they knew the family had received Germans in the house during the occupation. People were shot for less than that — women had their heads shaved, there were terrible goings-on, but a lot of aristocrats fraternized with the Germans; you could hardly blame them, after all, could you, Mademoiselle? Many of them were related. Why, the English royal family themselves were Germans, were they not? They had to change their name. There were intimate parties at the mill with Germans in attendance: elegant parties with music and dancing and interesting conversation, no doubt. He had served at table himself, and the Germans were always most correct, Mademoiselle, most correct, generous tippers.

"But, then, did she, after all, discover them and turn them in?" I asked.

"I'd rather not say more, Mademoiselle." He stood up politely as I rose to go and bowed his head and shook my hand with his damp, limp handshake.

16

THE SKY WAS SWEPT clear of clouds, as it was so often at that hour, the slow twilight of that place. Splashes of white light separated the long, shifting shadows on the lawn as the branches tossed restlessly in the wind. Moon roses, arum lilies, and milky daisies bowed their heads in the lingering evening heat. The odors of freshly mown grass and honeysuckle mingled with that of the stagnant, wearily seeping river.

On its banks my hosts were reclining in the shade of the willows. I stood and stared for a moment from a distance at their fine eighteenth-century faces, thinking that I would never see them again.

They lay side by side in the cream deck chairs Luis had set out for them on the lawn, their faces gleaming in the light. Madame's fine hair lay free on her shoulders. They were having cocktails. Their mellifluous voices and the clinking of the ice mingled harmoniously with the sighing of the wind in the leaves. They were attempting to throw their olive pits into the river, reaching back over their shoulders to cast them hard through the air, then watching them blown about by the wind, and pointing to where they landed, laughing like children.

Their childishness caught me off guard; it annoyed me. Was I not the child who should be having fun? From that distance they looked so youthful, carefree. They looked happy, one of those couples who are still miraculously happy, after so many years, whom everyone remarks upon. Did they dream one another's dreams? They did, they did.

When I approached, she placed her fingers on the sleeve of his blue shirt in a warning gesture. They both looked up with the same distant stare, narrowing their big, short-sighted eyes, as if they were puzzled that I would disturb them at their play. I could imagine her saying to him, "What does she want now, do you suppose? Haven't we done enough for her?"

And his replying, "Ah yes, but you know, with those North Americans or South Americans or South Africans, one never knows how they will behave." I was simply one in a long line of paying guests. How many had been necessary to maintain their happiness?

I began, "I will be leaving tonight after dinner. I just wanted to say good-bye. Luis will drive me to the bus stop in Pithiviers."

"Really! Luis to drive you to the bus stop?" Monsieur exclaimed. "Rather sudden, all of this, is it not?" he commented languidly, raising his thin eyebrows with a half smile, shifting his weight slightly, and throwing an olive pit into the river.

"It is time," I said fiercely. He put his hand into the pocket of his cream linen pants to jingle his change as they gathered themselves up.

I often had the feeling that they were able to communicate without words. A glance passed between them. It was enough to tell one another, "Oh, let her go. She has served her purpose, after all."

I trembled as I gave voice to that exchange. "I believe I have served my purpose here."

Madame made a wincing movement with her mouth and fussed with her collar. Monsieur responded more smoothly, "You have certainly learned to speak French remarkably well in a short time, my dear. We are both very proud of you."

The blood was beating in my head, and the clear light, coming through the trees along the river, glinted in my eyes, as I replied. "French! You think I have learned to speak French! What I have learned is to know you!"

Madame started as though she had been struck, rose from her chair, and walked nervously back and forth on the dry grass, leaning forward into the wind, her high heels sinking into the soil, her full skirt blowing against her thin legs. "Show us the self-control you have learned then, Deidre."

"I know what you wanted me for: a hot body to warm your cold bed," I cried.

Madame said, "Don't shout, Deidre."

"It is clear what you did: you took my letter, my money; you dressed me up like a doll for him; you made me a sacrificial lamb!" I shouted wildly over the jangling of Madame's gold bracelets as she moved her hands, smoothing her hair, the ruffle about her neck, the folds of her skirt.

Madame said coldly, "To exaggerate is to render insignificant. You have read all of this in some book. You read too much, my dear. Or perhaps you've seen it on the stage. You see yourself in some sort of melodrama, don't you? Sarah Bernhardt couldn't do better. You make yourself out to be a pathetic little victim in a bad play."

"I know what you are! I know what you did!" I screamed, my own words and the wind in the leaves and the slowly moving water all making me angrier.

Madame snapped, "What are you talking about now?"

It was Monsieur's turn to spring to his feet. He put his hand on his wife's arm and said, "You don't know how to talk to her, Catherine, let me do it." He came over to me, adopting a fatherly tone. "Dodo, listen, calm down," he said and tried to put his arm around my shoulders.

I pushed him away, exploding, "Don't you dare touch me! Who do you think I am — some sort of maid you can feel up whenever you like?"

Monsieur lowered his voice so that I could hardly hear him and whispered, "Don't you see you're making the situation impossible for me? How can I help you if you carry on in this way?" and his eyes glittered.

I waved my arms dramatically, my hair escaping from its pins and flying in my face and mouth. "I don't want your help. You have already taken everything from me: my affection, my body, my money . . ."

Monsieur backed off, and his blue eyes glinted coldly at me as he said, "Oh, so in the end it's a question of money, is it?"

"You're revolting," I said and hit him hard across his

soft cheek. I went on, "You are both revolting! You are Nazis! You had *Germans* in this house during the war."

Now it was Monsieur's turn to hesitate. He said, "Who told you that? What do you know of that business, anyway?"

Madame said, "Of course we had Germans here. They were aristocrats. The aristocracy is all one country. You wouldn't understand that."

I said, "And what about this? What about this?" and took the cameo from my pocket.

The couple stood and stared at one another. Monsieur said, "Where did she get that? Did you give it to her? I thought you lent it to her for the party."

Madame said sadly, "I did lend it to her. I thought it appropriate. She kept it."

I said, "It was you who stole it from those Jewish girls. Then you betrayed them, didn't you?"

Madame turned from me toward her husband, her face crimson. She said, "Where does she get such an idea? How does she know about —"

They faced one another in silence now, my presence suddenly forgotten. She waved her shaking hands in the air, and her lips trembled. The wind blew their hair about their faces as the water oozed on slowly between its gray, cracked banks.

Monsieur shrugged. "She's been talking to the servants, or to our professor or that fellow of hers."

Madame said, "She's heard something. You must have discussed the matter."

A tear rolled down her cheek. Her face was like wet stone. She clutched his arm and said, "Have you nothing to say? You know as well as I do what happened."

"The insinuations of a commoner, a mere child!" he said scornfully and shook himself loose of her.

She said, "Please, this isn't a question of class or age," and clung to his arm.

"Enough drama, for God's sake! None of this has any importance today," he shouted at her and looked at her with something resembling hate.

Madame began to plead softly. "It is very important to me."

"Damn it all, Catherine, leave me alone," he responded.

"Guy, please, tell her what really happened," she begged.

He lowered his voice and said, "You must know I can't do that, for God's sake. How could I ever do that to you?"

"What are you talking about? How can you insinuate something of the sort when you know perfectly well who betrayed those girls!" she exclaimed.

"Let it go, Catherine, for your own sake," he said.

"Guy, please, for my sake, admit the truth," she implored.

"Oh, I've had enough of you," he cried and strode off across the lawn. Madame sat down and wept silently, her back erect, staring before her with the tears slipping slowly down her pale cheeks like the river over the white stones. As they lost their composure, I gained mine. How ridiculous we all were.

Madame looked at me appraisingly, as though my outburst had given her new respect for me. Perhaps she decided it was wiser to take me into her confidence, to tell me what she knew. Or perhaps she told me what she thought I should hear. In any case this, more or less, is what I remember her telling me.

She had heard noises in the house one hot afternoon in the summer of '42. Guy had gone out again as usual, God knows where. She was lying down in my — the guest — room, because it was cooler, and she was nauseated again. She was almost five months pregnant, and she had been continuously nauseated. Every day and all day long, not just in the early mornings for the first few months, as they tell you it will be. "What they tell us women! The bill of goods they sell us!" she said in her old ironic, complicitous tone.

She was just looking for a cool place, like a cat, somewhere to stretch out and sleep. She had lain down on my bed beneath the window. She was lying there, tossing and turning, heavy and hot, despite the open windows, trying to sleep, wondering where Guy had gone, whom he was with this time. Then she heard noises above her. At first she thought she was imagining things. The walls of that old house are very thin, as I must have noticed. Sometimes the floorboards creaked with the wind. But the day was still.

She had climbed the stairs to the attic slowly and opened the door quietly. She stood there, as pregnant women do, awkwardly, even before their bellies are swollen, one hand on her back, her silk gown sticking to her skin, like the ironers in that painting by Degas, did I know the one she meant?

She had seen them before they saw her. They were sitting opposite one another on the bed, cross-legged, in a ray of sunlight, which came in aslant from the small, high window: two young girls, two beauties. They had not closed the bed curtain. Their heads had apparently been shaved, but the hair had begun to grow back in short, uneven tufts. Their heads had such a pretty oval shape. Delft blue veins coursed through their pale feet.

One of them was a redhead, with the calm milky skin and freckles that accompany that savage color. The other was dark-haired. They were playing cards, quite coolly, she told me, as though they had lived there all their lives. Guy must have given them a pack of their good English playing cards, the blue-and-red kind with the bicycles on them. The older girl was even wearing one of Madame's old sundresses, rather a good one, actually, striped black and white, a dress that she had worn as a girl.

When they first looked up, their eyes were warm and welcoming — excited, as though they were waiting for something: another gift. How well she knew that look! They must have thought it was her husband coming to them.

"What are you doing here?" she asked them. She was suddenly in a rage, feeling the blood rush to her head and so nauseated she felt she must throw up then and there. The girls jumped up and stammered something, trembling like trapped fawns.

She walked over to them, threw back the bed curtain, pulled off the counterpane. There were magazines and tins of food, an enamel jug for water, a chamber pot, hidden up there under the bed. They must have been there for quite a while, and they looked well-installed, comfortable. She might never have found them if they had kept the curtain completely drawn, but they must have grown careless, feeling safe up there, or desperate. Even when she shouted at them, went over to them and gave each a slap on the face, they did not try to run away from her.

She was furious, she said, not because of what Guy had done — she knew immediately he had brought them up there: it was something she might have done herself, after all, hiding two pretty children from the police — but because of his keeping it a secret from her. Had he not trusted her by then? What did she care what he did with them there?

They had been married for more than ten years when this happened, and she had seen him with other women, how he watched them, all the young ones, particularly the very young ones. He had developed what she called the irresistible taste for fresh bread.

I looked at her. "So you called the police out of anger at him? And you took their jewelry as a keepsake, besides!" I said, accusingly.

She looked sadly at me. "Still so naïve. I see you have not learned much with us after all." She sighed. "People like us put honor above everything else. We believe above all in loyalty."

"Here, take this back," I responded and tried to thrust the cameo into her hand. She brushed my hand away impatiently, and the cameo fell to the ground. I bent over and picked it up.

She said, "You are not looking for the truth. You want things to be simple, and they are not. You want Guy to choose between us, as if that were ever a choice he would consider. And as for those girls, who betrayed them, why don't you ask him?"

"I will talk to him now," I said in a small voice, shifting and squaring my shoulders. But my knees grew so watery I could hardly stand.

The wind filled the short sleeves of her light-colored dress like little wings. She said, "Why didn't you ask me directly what you wanted to know, dear? I would have told you the truth. Why go behind my back?"

17

I SAW DOLORES draw aside the lace curtain in her cottage window and watch as Monsieur and I walked down the driveway. The hunting season, which had begun a few days after our return from the castle country, was now in full swing. We could hear the sound of guns in the distance as we walked up the dust path. It seemed to make Monsieur even more restless. He walked beside me in his khaki hunting jacket with its innumerable pockets, his arms folded, his hands clutched under his arms, his shoulders unusually hunched. But nothing was going to stop me from getting what I wanted, at last. I walked beside him in silence in the twilight, holding myself erect, not touching his arm, groping around for my anger, but feeling his proximity breathlessly with every part of my body.

Monsieur did not seem to know what to do with me, for once. He bent his head toward me and began, "I know you understand why it hasn't been possible for us to see one another recently. It must have been very painful for you, surely. Of course you would wish to leave us."

There was nothing I could say to that, so I walked on ahead of him with the wind blowing my hair around my face. He caught up and took my hand, exclaiming, "What a little savage you are!" When he touched me, I felt myself flush. I withdrew my hand. He tried harder, speaking gently. "Look, do you want me to abandon Catherine, take you off somewhere? Think about it. What would become of her? You don't realize how fragile she is. She has seen psychiatrists, doctors. She just told me about that new man in Paris. But none of them has ever been able to help her: I am her whole world. Without me I don't think she could go on. Even now with her denial of complicity in this terrible business: what would you have me do? She has never recovered from what happened to those children, from her miscarriage. Her life has been terribly sad. If you must blame anyone, you must blame us together."

I wanted to say, "Forget those children, forget the past," but Madame was right: I did want things to be simple; I did want him to choose. "Did you assume she had called the police? Did you ever ask her about it?" I asked him. He said nothing, walking on now a little ahead of me with his hands in the pockets of his hunting jacket, the collar turned up against the wind.

"She just denied calling them herself. Is that the truth, after all?" I asked him. And then, as he stared back at me, tears glistening in his eyes, and put his arm around my shoulders, I thought: But *he* is the one who called the police, who betrayed the girls, or if he did not call the police himself, he must have condoned her doing it. She only did what he wanted her to do. Once he had had enough of them, he would have wanted to get rid of them, just as he wants to get rid of me, now.

We were entering the forest and passed a group of hunters with their gray hats and their little folding stools going the other way. "Perhaps we should turn back now, enough has happened," Monsieur said sadly.

"No, I want to go on," I found myself saying. My brain was working clearly now. I took Monsieur's arm and leaned against him, feeling the extraordinary comfort and warmth of his body beside me. I could hear his labored breathing, and from time to time I looked up at his face in profile, the straight nose, his full glistening lips.

It was September, and leaves the colors of amber and cinnamon were falling from the windswept branches. I was warmed by the exercise, the fading sunlight, Monsieur's acquiescence.

Madame's presence was there as well; her presence on my body, her makeup on my face, her taste in the clothes I was wearing. I could feel her fingers stroke my hand. The words I spoke were her words. Had I not learned them from her? Was my way of expressing myself not her way of seeing the world?

The two girls were also there. They would always be with me now, their words coming to me clearly, as though they were mine.

> *Where did you get that lipstick?*
> *He gave it to me.*
> *Let me borrow some.*
> *No. You're too young for lipstick.*

But not too young to do what I do with him?
You don't really do anything.
Yes I do, I do.

We come to a small clearing. The leaves lie heaped on the ground. I hear the sound of beating wings, the crack of a gun. The dog is sniffing and digging ecstatically in the earth. I turn to Monsieur and cannot help gazing at him, the evening light in his hair.

"I need to see you naked, now. Take off your clothes," I order him, and I reach to lift his shirt out of his trousers, to undo his fly.

I pull at his shirt so recklessly that a button snaps.

"Such violence! What about the hunters?" he says, but I know that he will. I unbutton my shirt, step out of my jeans fast, letting them drop to the ground. We fall together into the leaves. I lie on top of him, pinning his legs, feeling his slender body, the slight swell of his stomach, the broad back, the surge of his lust. As he shuts his eyes against the glare, my tongue enters his mouth. I cup his head in my hands. I smell the earth and the pine. I run my hands through the feathers of his hair. I grow light. I am flying through the forest, through the beech and the pine, dipping and rising through the dusk. I hear the keening of the wind in the leaves, the evensong of birds, the hum of a bee, the report of a hunter's gun. I think: Whatever happens later, I have this, this and this.

When he fell asleep, I lay awake, looking up at the sky at the darkness pouring down through the trees, and the moon on its slow walk, followed by the stars. I had barely drifted off, when at dawn I was woken by pure thunder. During the night a storm had risen. Sharp cracks were followed by long rolls, as if the sky had split open. Heavy drops of rain fell, warm on my forehead and cheeks. Then he put his arms around my neck and I looked up into the dark blur of his face.

He said, "Catherine will be missing us, you know."

I said, "No, she'll still be asleep." He entered me again as the rain came down onto our naked bodies like a waterfall, bringing sweet release. The grass bent, and the laurels dipped before us. I thought of our lovemaking as electric, magic, like Prospero's tempest, which opened up a brave, new world for Miranda.

While still at some distance from the house, we heard the cry. It sounded like a wild animal caught in a trap. Then I recognized Dolores's voice, and Madame's face flashed before me. I recalled my promise never to leave her alone at night. "It's the river," she was saying, and I saw a bird swooping down, its belly gray.

Then Dolores saw us returning and rushed up toward us, flapping her apron before her, the rain falling on her smooth, round face. "It's Madame! Madame! Madame!" she screamed. "Madame is dead!"

We found her lying in the bath, the same bath where she had bathed me so carefully on my birthday. There was even the same odor of lavender bath salts, but mingled now with urine and the smell of the drains, which always smelled when it rained. Madame had poured bath salts into the water but had not flushed the toilet. Her small white body was lying so tranquilly in its pink pool, head thrown back over the edge of the tub, arms spread out as if stretching lazily, hands dangling languidly, that, for a moment, I thought Dolores, with her usual hysteria, had exaggerated. Madame was not dead, she had simply fallen asleep in her rose-colored bath. Perhaps Monsieur thought the same thing, for he, too, stood there as though mesmerized, unable to move. For a moment we stood side by side in silence. Nothing moved except the rain against the window. Madame's eyes were open, fixed. I waited for them to blink.

Then Dolores shattered the early morning quiet. She entered the room, panting and wailing and flapping her apron, and I noticed the blood seeping from the deep gashes in Madame's wrists and the razor on the bath mat. Madame had cut her wrists deeply and had lacerated her ankles, too, using Monsieur's razor. The rain was hammering against the panes of the bathroom window, and the dog was howling outside.

Monsieur bent down and put two fingers to the side of Madame's neck. He said, "Got to get her out of the warm water," and lifted her with one movement — he was a surprisingly strong man, stepping back from the bath with her head falling over his arm, her wet hair hanging down, blood and water pouring all over the floor. As he lifted her, and the water fell from her, her mouth opened, and she gave a faint moan. Her very white skin looked almost blue, and stretch marks scarred her stomach and her breasts, which hung down slackly. I could see she was even older and much frailer than I had imagined.

"I need towels fast; make a tourniquet," Monsieur shouted at me, as I stood, staring.

While he held Madame sprawled on his lap, like a reverse pietà, we made tourniquets around her arms and bound the gashes on her wrists and ankles with towels and covered her body with a blanket. She had cut a deeper gash in her left wrist than in the right, and the blood flowed from the cut. Her ankles were cut less profoundly.

"Get Luis and the car," Monsieur shouted, rising and pushing Dolores out of the way with a shoulder. I helped him carry Madame down the front stairs, where I had first seen her, water and blood dripping behind us as we went. In the rain we carried her out into the courtyard with Dolores hovering at her side, trying to cover her body with a big black umbrella and with the dark dog howling by her side.

We placed her on the backseat of the Citroën, and I crouched with her head on my lap beside Monsieur, who cradled her body with an expression of stunned rage on his face. I was not sure with whom he was in a rage: himself or me or perhaps just life. I would have preferred if he had wept or cried out, loudly, but he said nothing, only staring angrily before him in silence, and all the while her dark blood seeped fast through the white towels.

Luis drove slowly along the wet, winding road, the windshield wipers beating back and forth constantly. Why was Luis, who always drove too fast, incapable of speeding now? Was it shock that had frozen him? It was not shock.

"Hurry up, for God's sake, put your foot on the gas," Monsieur barked. It must have been the only time anyone had ever asked Luis to drive faster.

In the hospital Monsieur and I were asked to wait in the waiting room for the doctor's verdict, sitting in stunned silence on orange plastic chairs beside a potted plant with waxy green leaves. From time to time a doctor would emerge and explain something in fast French. I was hardly able to understand, as if all the French I had learned with Madame had now suddenly left with her. I gathered only that they were doing what they could: they had stitched up her wounds; she had received more than thirty stitches. She had lost a great deal of blood; she had cut a main artery; she was receiving a transfusion; they were trying to resuscitate her.

We must wait.

From time to time Monsieur muttered to me or perhaps himself, almost incomprehensibly. "One day, she will succeed," he said. I did not really understand what he was talking about at the time. Later, I learned that this was not the first time Madame had attempted to take her life. She had tried gas; she had used sleeping pills; she had even attempted to drown herself by jumping into the river, stones in her pockets, after she lost the baby.

But at the time Monsieur's words meant little to me. I was dazed, conscious only of sensations: the hard seat where I sat, the pricking of a rash on my legs, fatigue, the smell of my body after sex, of Madame's blood on me, the shiny, waxy leaves of the plant beside me, rain, which had turned to a dull drizzle and continued to fall outside, and a voice in my head, which kept muttering, Please, God, don't let her die, don't let her die.

Sometime that afternoon, I heard my voice suggesting I go and get something for Monsieur to eat. He said, lifting his head from his hands, always automatically polite, "There must be someplace to eat around here. You ought to eat, yourself."

"I think I saw a sign for a cafeteria in the basement."

We took the elevator down into the basement, standing side by side in silence. The walls were green, the pipes visible. We passed a room where women were ironing sheets. I thought of the Degas painting Madame had mentioned, women putting their hands to their backs, yawning. I, too, felt terribly tired. We had been waiting all day. We had hardly slept all night.

Should I make a pact with God? If Madame lived, I would give up my lover. I would not make a pact. There was no need to make a pact. It was far too easy. I felt no desire for this man beside me. He looked old, ancient. There were dark bags under his eyes, and in the bags someone seemed to have cut lines. I hardly recognized him.

Instead, I ate a ham sandwich and drank a cup of milk tea and sat opposite him in silence and listened to the rain, the voice going on and on in my head: Please don't let her die.

As Monsieur sipped the tea I had bought him, he looked up at me, as though he were noticing me for the first time since we had found Madame in the bath. He sniffed slightly. He said, "You need to go home and wash and change your clothes." It was true. I needed a bath. I smelled strongly of sex and dry leaves and Madame's blood, which had seeped into my clothes, my skin, it seemed into my own veins.

When I arrived at the mill, I wanted to call someone, anyone. I wanted to call Richard or Cecile or even the Hawthornes in the château, but Dolores was waiting for me in the hall with a basket of fresh laundry in her arms and the offer of an apple pie, the apple slices placed in neat concentric rings, still hot on the kitchen counter. Dolores, at any moment of crisis, baked, and that day it was an apple pie. I wanted to tell her to leave me alone, but I could not because of the pie, which she maintained she had made just for me.

In the kitchen, over the pie, Dolores shrieked, "Oh, oh, Madame, Madame! How is she? Will she be all right? What did the doctor say?"

I mumbled something vague.

She was relentless. "I knew she knew what was happening. I was afraid something like this would happen to her. She couldn't bear to be left all alone in the house at night. She told you never to leave her alone in the house, didn't she? How could you go off with the baron? What if she dies?" And Dolores stared at me, as if willing me to weep or scream or tear my hair with grief. I felt she wanted me to apologize to her, to fall on my knees. Above all, she wanted me to promise to give up Monsieur. But I was not going to give her that satisfaction.

Dolores clutched her stomach, pulled at her thinning hair, and squinted wildly. She moaned, "Ah! Ah! What will become of us? Where will we go? We will lose our land, our lovely house on the hill. After I had saved poor Madame, made sure she was safe for so many years, kept it all a secret," she said dramatically.

"So you knew?" I asked, the outlines of those events beginning to emerge for me, now, for the first time.

Are you sure L. has sent our packages to Papa?

We can only hope he has.

What if he has kept our things for himself or given Mother's jewelry to his wife? He's always talking about his wife.

Dolores went on: "Oh! Oh! Such a terrible sight, poor Madame in her bath in the water, floating, just like those children, drowned."

"Drowned?" I said, looking up at her and thinking of my dream, the soft arms dragging me down and down into the depths.

"Poor Madame in the water. She was frightened of the water, the river. How could you and Monsieur leave her alone all night?"

"What are you talking about, Dolores? Madame didn't drown. She cut herself in the bath," I said rudely.

"You knew what would happen."

"That's enough, Dolores," I reproached her and rose and turned my back on her.

Dolores helped herself to another piece of apple pie and dropped it on her plate. She drew herself up. "What I suffered for poor Madame, so that she would be safe, so that her baby would be safe, so that my Luis would be safe.

What I suffered, my head, my stomach, now all in vain."
She chewed, reflecting on her suffering. "How was I to
know those children would act so foolishly?" she asked me.

I looked at her and asked, "What did they do?"

She said, "They must have had lice in their hair, that's
why it had been cut off. They had little curls, reddish or
black maybe. Couldn't swim, of course. Girls like that can't
swim. Hysterical. That's the way their people are, hysterical, out of control." She pulled at her own hair wildly.

"At first, Luis let me believe it was Madame who called
the police."

Dolores looked at me and said, "I don't know what my
Luis told you, but he is always loyal."

I took a chance: "Then he told me it was you."

"Why were you putting your nose into things that did
not concern you? Why were you stirring up trouble? Why
were you trying to find out what Madame had done? Why
could you not leave things unsaid?" Dolores demanded.

"How could you all do such a terrible thing?" I asked her.

She stared out the window and said, "Charity begins at
home, Mademoiselle; you will find out when you have
one — if you ever have one, which I'm beginning to
doubt. I wanted to save Madame from the police. I wanted
to save her from Monsieur, who was all the time going up
and down those stairs. And I didn't like my Luis going up
into that attic all the time, either. Running up and down
those steps with food for those foreigners, when there
wasn't enough in the house for us! Why should he have
had to do that? Risking his life and my life. I ask you, why?
Wearing himself out, running himself ragged. How was I

to know what would happen to those girls?" She went on in her rambling way. "Dresses ballooning and all the little tufts of hair floating around their heads."

I saw them then, Anna and Lea looking out the attic window and watching the van coming down the dust path, the gendarmes climbing out in their cloaks, the clack of the van's doors, all in slow motion as though it were a dream.

This time they know their mother was wrong. They know what will happen. I see Anna grasping Lea by the hand and telling her to follow, leading her out of the room. They run down the slippery back stairs I had run down so many times. They run across the stones of the patio, the direct sunlight suddenly bright in their eyes, gleaming on their pale legs, lighting up the blue veins in their bare feet, the wind blowing their thin dresses against their bodies and tossing the little tufts of hair like new buds about their heads. They feel the sun on their bare shoulders, hear the waters rolling with their soft murmur, the rooks caw-cawing, see a bird swooping down over the water, the bright butterflies hovering above the moon roses, the maiden fern, the silver willows, straight and tall, stirring up the smooth blue sky. They feel light, and their heads are spinning, as though they are flying into the smooth, blue sky. They are hollowed, emptied out, and all the world's loveliness is entering into them. They are part of the light and the sun and the air and one another. They are holding hands and plunging into the cold water, throwing themselves into the river with a great forward leap.

It all comes back to them: they are coming home from school, walking down the Rue des Rosiers with their heavy satchels on their backs as the sun sinks. They are looking up at the open shutters and windows on the fourth floor; they can hear the radio playing a song. Charles Trenet is singing. They are running up the stairs, and Maman's face is in the open door, her hair parted on the side, loose and dark on her shoulders, her apron with the frilled edge tied around her neck. Papa is there, too, in the shadows behind her, and they can smell the odor of freshly baked apples. The table is set with the blue bowls and the gray jug of frothed milk and the dark chocolate box with the pink dancer painted on the lid. There is a light behind their mother, and she clasps them in her arms.

I see the dresses filled with air, the faces down in the water, the tufts of hair floating on the surface.

Dolores and I watched from the window as the black Citroën came slowly down the dust path, the high beams piercing the dark and lighting up the courtyard and the creeper-covered house. We heard the wheels crunch the pebbles of the courtyard. Luis opened the car door for Monsieur, and he stepped out. He grasped Luis's hand and leaned on his arm, as Madame had so often leaned on his. Monsieur was bent toward Luis, talking to him earnestly as they walked slowly across the courtyard and back into the house. The taller, blond baron was leaning on the younger, dark-haired man. They looked, I thought, as they stood in the doorway together, like a couple.

I stood in the low-ceilinged hallway with Dolores hovering behind me, watching as they entered the house together just as Madame and Monsieur had so many times.

With the night behind them and their shadows before them in the dimly lit hall, I saw how old the baron was. I thought, But he must be sixty, over sixty, surely. I did not expect this old man to speak to me, and indeed he said nothing but glanced at me with his haughty blue gaze, as though he did not recognize me, as though my awkward presence were an intrusion in his house. There was nothing to say. I watched as Luis helped him climb up the stairs to his bedroom, slowly, without Madame.

18

ONLY THE DOG came to say good-bye to me, as I
stood in the courtyard with my backpack, waiting
for Luis to start the car, staring down at the shallow autumn stream, which was hardly moving over the
cold, moss-covered stones. Little ripples, shadows of ripples, slipped between gray, caked banks. A cluster of leaves
floated on its surface, turning round and round. There was
the faint odor of stagnant water mingled with that of late-
blooming roses.

I knelt down and clasped the dog against me and
thought of the words I had read.

*Funny, isn't it, to think of all the animals running free in
the fresh air, and of the two of us caged up here, in this
attic.*

I let him jump all over me, licking my face and hands passionately, until Dolores emerged from the cottage and led
him away, dragging him, growling, over the stones behind
her, his tail between his legs.

I climbed into the car in my blue jeans and flat shoes and

sat in the front seat with my backpack between me and
Luis. I turned my head as we drove up the dust path and
looked back at the old creeper-covered house. It was twilight, the sun was sinking, and the trees were already dark
and rustled in the wind. The evening sounded with the
wind and beating wings and frogs croaking hoarsely in the
dry riverbed. No lights gleamed in the windows of the
house.

I watched it disappear gradually. Then we were driving
fast through the flat wheat fields of the Beauce, which had
fed the country for so many centuries.

I would soon be leaving this ancient country. It had
brought forth so many great and generous ideas, which
themselves had spawned dreams of freedom and equality
in so many places around the globe. I remembered the
French women from the châteaux I had seen: Agnès Sorel, the Mistress of Blois, Louise de Lorraine, Diane de
Poitiers, and all the rest.

I thought of the great kings who had built up a strong
centralized country where all the schoolchildren read from
the same schoolbook at the same hour; I thought of the
great writers I had read that summer who had created
imaginary worlds for me to wander in.

It was a country that had given birth to revolutions,
codes of law, and ways of living well. And it had brought
forth war and destruction and the camp at Pithiviers. I saw
the children struggle along, two by two, holding hands,
singing as they went, because they had been told they were
going at last to join their mothers.

Madame's body had been taken up to Paris, where she

would be buried in the family mausoleum in the Père-Lachaise cemetery. Monsieur, dressed in black, his face a poppy red, would accompany her on the train. Without her there to allow him to live out his fantasies, he would not last long.

I reached into the pocket of my jeans and pulled out the cameo. "You gave this to Madame, did you not, to implicate her? You wanted her tainted with what you had stolen, didn't you?" I asked Luis.

He glanced at me but said nothing for a while. Then he said, "You are a spoiled girl who understands nothing. Dolores gave the girls' cameo to Madame because she loved her."

I burst out, "You never sent the girls' jewelry to their father in Paris? You never sent on their letters or mine? You knew all along that it was Dolores who had called the police, and you deliberately misled me!"

Luis said, "You ask too many questions, Mademoiselle. Had you been less curious, no one would have been hurt, yourself included. But once you began to inquire, it became necessary for me to protect our position as best I could."

"Madame would still be here if you had told me the truth."

He said, in his honeyed tones, very gently, "If you will allow me to put it bluntly, Mademoiselle, you heard what you wanted to hear, and you did what you wanted to do with the information. Perhaps had you been less quick to accuse, to exaggerate —"

I remembered Madame saying, "To exaggerate is to render insignificant."

Perhaps she was right: I had not cared for either her or Monsieur. I had seen them first as resembling the heroes and heroines of the books I was reading, and then as the villains, but never as they were, as I was, with all our petty hates and jealousies, our vanity and our miserable groping for love and happiness.

The girls, too, trapped as they were and awaiting with fear their tragic destiny, were preoccupied by the same everyday preoccupations. They had tried so hard to be good. They had been so full of hope.

Their words came to me then:

Do you remember the little boy who kept saying he was Benjamin's brother? He had forgotten his own name, and all he could remember to say was, I am Benjamin's brother.

ACKNOWLEDGMENTS

The following works were invaluable in the writing of this book: Serge Klarsfeld's *French Children of the Holocaust,* Michael Marrus and Robert Paxton's *Vichy France and the Jews,* Philippe Burrin's *France Under the Germans,* Laurel Holliday's anthology *Children in the Holocaust and World War II: Their Secret Diaries,* Paul Webster's *Pétain's Crime: The Complete Story of French Collaboration in the Holocaust;* Claude Morhange-Bégué's *Chamberet: Recollections from an Ordinary Childhood;* Eric Conan's *Sans Oublier les Enfants,* Colonel Rémy's *Mémoires d'un agent secret de la France libre.*

Thanks to the following for the help they gave me in the research and writing of this book: Jeannette and Bernard Perrette, Victoria Redel, Terese Svoboda, Ronnie Sharfman, Diane de Sanders, Sondra Olsen, Gay Walley, particularly Leigh-Ann Eubanks in Ithaca, New York, for her excellent help with the bibliography, Ben Voyles and Lily Tuck.

Amy Hempel for her support and generosity.

My agent, Robin Strauss.

And always with great gratitude for my beloved Bill, without whom this book would never have been written.

For my three wonderful girls: Sasha, Cybele, and Brett, who were fortunate enough to know Pithiviers in a time of peace.